POISONED PROSE

THE ACCIDENTAL MEDIUM BOOK TWO

AMY BOYLES

LADYBUGBOOKS LLC

CHAPTER 1

I stared at my sister, who had just knocked on my door. I hadn't seen her in three years and had only spoken to her a handful of times since. So saying that I was surprised was an understatement.

She ran her fingers through her dyed jet-black hair and pulled a pair of lime-green-framed sunglasses from her eyes. "What? Don't I at least get a hug?"

I moved in for an awkward embrace. "I'm just so…surprised to see you here. What are you doing?"

My gaze darted nervously to Snow, the ghost standing in the corner of the cabin. She nodded at the heaping gym bag that Cammie dropped on the floor. "If I didn't know any better, I'd say that your sister is moving in."

No. No. No. No. No. My sister couldn't stay here. Everywhere that Cammie went, bad things happened.

To me.

"Nice place you got here," she said, dropping onto the couch and kicking her feet up. "Where should I sleep? You got two bedrooms?"

I grabbed her feet and dropped them onto the floor. "No. There's only one bedroom and it's mine. All mine. You can't stay here, Cammie. I've got…" *Think, Paige. Come up with something, anything that will convince her to go.* "Cammie, look. There's this book that I need to get to my agent. I'm in a bind, see. If I don't write it, the publisher may void my contract and I'll be broke."

She gave me a stare full of pity. "I heard Walter already took your money. So you're broke anyway."

"Yes, but I'll be *more* broke if you stay. You know how it is when I write. I can't talk to people or have anyone around. I need all my focus so that I can conjure the story."

"Trust me, you won't even know that I'm here."

She nestled farther back onto the couch. I could not let my sister get too comfortable. We were oil and water, you see, and didn't get along. Not because we hadn't tried. We just never saw eye to eye. And if I was honest, I supposed there was some jealousy in our relationship as I'd become a once-successful author. *Once* being the primary adjective.

"Cammie, seriously. Don't you have a third husband to get to? Or a job that needs help?"

"Nah, I took a vacation. When I saw in the paper that Walter was dead and found out that you were staying here at Willow Lake, I just knew that I had to come visit. Oh, Paige, we are gonna have so much fun doing stuff like fishing and boat riding. We're gonna have ourselves a little vacation. But if you don't mind, right now I'm dead tired." She yawned for emphasis. "Just let me catch a few winks of sleep and then we can hit the town, and maybe I can catch me a good-looking rich man."

Oh God. It was worse than I thought. She wanted to stay. For days. "Listen, Cammie, all of that sounds great, but maybe another time. Like, after I have this book written." I laughed, trying to make light of a situation that was terribly heavy. "Writing is so time-consuming. There's no room for anything or *anyone* else."

"Nonsense. You'll make time for me."

Of course I would. This was just so quintessential Cammie, expecting people to bow down to her every whim.

"As much as I'd love for you to stay, I just don't think now's a good time."

But her eyes were closed. She wasn't even listening.

"Looks like you're stuck with her," Snow told me. "I'll let y'all catch up. See you in a bit."

Though I wanted to shout for Snow to come back and save me, the truth was, Cammie couldn't see spirits. Attempting to explain my recently acquired ability to communicate with the dead wasn't exactly high on my bucket list.

"You doing okay?" she asked. Apparently my sister wasn't already asleep. "You look like you just seen a ghost."

"Yeah, I'm fine. But listen, maybe we can put you up in a hotel or something."

She tsked. "I cain't ask my baby sister to put out any money for me. 'Sides, you got your own problems, what with Walter taking you to the cleaners and all. What a jerk. I always hated that SOB."

"Cammie!"

"What?" She shrugged. "The truth's the truth. Now, I'm just going to get a little shut-eye, and when I wake up, we can catch up and hang out."

"I don't think…"

"You don't think what?"

That it's the right time for us to catch up? How the heck could I explain to my sister that I'd been conked on the head by a magical book, could now see spirits and work magic, and that I was also on the hunt for said magical book because it had disappeared after falling on my noggin.

When I didn't answer, she glared at me. "You ain't gonna play that I'm-better-than-you card, are you?"

"What?" I plastered a hand to my chest. "No, I would never do that."

She looked at me a long time before nodding. "Good. Because we're sisters and Mama would want us to be together. I'll only stay a few days. Just long enough for us to have some fun. You know, like the good old days."

What good old days? Did she mean the ones when she would break a window and blame it on me? Or was she talking about when she accidentally kissed my boyfriend in the closet while we were playing spin the bottle? Just which good old days was my sister referring to?

But right as I was about to ask her, the sound of soft snoring filled the cabin. Great. She was asleep.

Then I remembered that I had a date with Grim that night. Oh crap. If Cammie laid her gaze on him, she'd want to steal him from me.

Well, I couldn't let that happen, now could I?

CHAPTER 2

"So how're things going with your sis?" Snow asked a little while later.

Cammie had fallen into slumber so relaxed that her snores filled the cabin to the point where the walls nearly shook from the vibrations.

"She's fine," I said, slipping into an emerald-green jumpsuit. "What do you think of this?"

Snow smirked. "She's fine as in, 'She's fine,' or she's fine as in, you're dealing with it."

"I'm dealing with it and considering calling Grim and canceling tonight."

Snow gasped. "And deprive yourself of the chance to stare at him for hours on end? How could you do that to me?"

I giggled. "Don't you mean, how could I do that to myself? Because if my sister sees him, she'll want to sink her claws into his flesh. It's always been like that between us. She's so competitive. In high school if a guy showed any interest in me, she was suddenly flirting with him, telling him how good-looking he was. I can't tell you how many boys suddenly stopped calling me and started calling her because of it."

"She sounds like a terrible sister."

"And yet she's on my couch wanting to spend quality time with me."

I took a pair of gold hoops and placed them to my ears. "Do you like these ones or the emeralds?"

"The emeralds," she said. "Match the culottes."

They weren't culottes, but whatever. I picked up a small pair of emerald studs and pushed the poles through my ears. My mind drifted back to Cammie on the couch. Maybe she would be sleeping when Grim arrived and I could sneak outside to meet him.

Or perhaps I could figure out a way to put her under a spell so that she wouldn't wake up for, say, five hundred hours.

"Maybe she's changed," Snow offered from her spot atop the bed. "Maybe she wants to make amends for all the wrongs that she did to you."

"Perhaps." That was a possibility, and one that filled me with hope. Certainly Cammie wasn't still as immature as she was when we'd been growing up. Surely she'd matured some. After all, it wasn't as if we were still in high school.

"Paige," she called from the living room.

"Sounds like Sleeping Beauty has awoken," Snow joked.

"You say that because you think it's funny." I grabbed my clutch and pointed it at her. "It won't be funny when she goes after your boyfriend."

"My boyfriend, if I even had one, would be dead."

"You think that'll stop her? Nothing stops my sister."

"Paige, come out here! There's a hot guy on a bike out front of the cabin. I think he's lost. Do you think we could get him to undress for us?"

I rolled my eyes. Nope. It didn't appear as if anything had changed. I exited the bedroom with my clutch under my arm.

"No, he won't undress for us," I snapped. "And get away from that window. You'll freak him out."

Cammie begrudgingly dropped the curtain. "Why're you all dressed up? And who were you talking to a minute ago?"

"I was on my phone."

"You're not holding it."

I rolled my eyes and dug through my purse. "It's in here."

Cammie pointed to the kitchen counter. "It's over there."

"So it is." I laughed as if to say, *Silly me*, and slipped the phone into the clutch. "I was talking on my new smart watch."

"That looks like a Timex."

I clasped a hand over the face. "That's what you think. These smart watches nowadays look just like a good old Timex. Takes a licking and keeps on ticking, you know?"

Her gaze washed up and down me with suspicion. "There's something different about you."

Everything is different about me. "I have no idea what you're talking about."

The doorbell rang. Crap. Any hope I had of sneaking away without Cammie having a chance to interrogate Grim had vanished.

I moved to the door and blocked her from answering. Then I whirled around and said in my sharpest, most intimidating voice, "This is my date. Cammie, do not do anything to embarrass me."

"Like what?"

"Like lift your skirt over your head."

She crossed her arms and jutted out a hip. "I'm not even wearing a skirt."

"That's never stopped you before. Now. Promise to be on your best behavior?"

"I guess." I waited for a better answer and she shrugged. "Fine. Best behavior. Cross my heart."

"Be prepared to stick a needle in your eye if you lie."

She smirked. "Just open the door."

I did so and smiled. Grim wore a dark charcoal suit with a lighter gray tie, crisp white shirt and had his hair pulled back. His appearance literally stole my breath.

"Hi," I whispered.

"Hi, yourself." He pulled a bouquet of white roses from behind him and handed them to me. "You look beautiful."

"So do you. I mean handsome. You look so handsome."

"Hey there," Cammie said, invading Grim's line of sight. "I'm Cammie. Paige's sister."

Why did she have to be here? "Yes," I said. "This is my sister, Grim. She's come to visit for a few hours."

"Days to weeks," Cammie corrected.

Grim took her hand in that way that Southern men shake a woman's hand—not vertically like they do other men, but horizontally as if she's a lady, fingers and back of the hand up, palm down.

I had no idea that Grim possessed such good manners. His mother raised him right.

"My, my, I like you," Cammie said, eyes glittering. "You got a brother?"

He chuckled. "I'm afraid there's only me."

"Well, if things don't work out with my sister, I'll be happy to give you my number."

I may have accidentally-on-purpose stomped on Cammie's foot. She howled and I said apologetically, "Oh my gosh! I'm so sorry. I didn't see your foot there."

Cammie glared. "It hadn't moved in a good ten seconds."

"Well, I must be suffering from blindness that only occurs from the waist down."

Cammie eyed Grim hungrily. "I don't have any problems seeing below the waist."

"Okay, well, then." I pushed Grim forward. "We should get going, right? We don't want to be late for dinner."

But really, I didn't want Grim to succumb to Cammie. Even though her manners were on the grotesque side, she had big long eyelashes and huge boobs. They were even bigger now than they were three years ago. Men flocked to her. Or they used to. I wasn't about to let Grim fall under her strange, classless spell.

"Yes, we don't want to be late," Grim said, offering his arm.

It was such a sweet gesture, and it took me by surprise.

I held out the flowers to, who took them. "Well, what are you doing just standing there?" she griped. "Take the man's arm. Let him escort you to his Harley Davidson Heritage Classic with its twin engines."

Grim lifted a brow. "You're familiar with my bike?"

"I've been on the back of more bikes than I can count. Yeah, I know my way around a Harley."

"I'll have to take you for a ride sometime."

Cammie smiled and my heart sank. "That would be great."

I practically yanked Grim out the door. "Okay, well, don't wait up. I'll be back later."

Cammie just smiled. "See you then."

We stepped outside and I yanked the door closed. It slammed shut, and I blew my bangs from my eyes. "Guess I don't know my own strength."

Grim didn't say anything. He just looked down at me and smiled.

And my heart melted.

~

"I DIDN'T KNOW you had a sister," he said after we'd been seated and had ordered dinner.

"Neither did I," I joked. "But yep, I've got one, and she's quite the character."

His eyes twinkled with amusement. "I take it that y'all aren't close."

"Well, considering that she just showed up at the cabin today unannounced, I would say that you're right."

He lifted a brow. "Huh. Sounds like there's a story there."

"I'm not sure if there's a story any more than we're just talking about Cammie and that's how she is—just shows up with a suitcase and expects the world to bow down to her."

"If I had a brother, I'd be glad to spend some time with him, whether it was an inconvenience or not."

I deflated onto the back of the chair. "I sound like a brat, don't I?"

"You sound like someone under stress."

There, he was one-hundred-percent right. I was broke and had hit a wall in the book that I was writing. I didn't have any idea of where to go next in the story.

I pushed a smile onto my face. "Stress? I have no idea what you're talking about. That word isn't even in my vocabulary."

Grim reached over and took my hand. A chill snaked from my arm to my spine. "If there's one thing that I would like to do for you, it's alleviate your stress."

And I would let you do it. There was something about growing older— I had no interest in wasting any time, especially when it came to men. If Grim was into getting down and dirty, I might not care enough to stop it from happening.

Oh God. I could just sense my mother rolling over in her grave. She would have killed me if I thought in such a way. But she wasn't here, so I could think however I wanted.

I smiled widely at Grim. He glanced up as I caught sight of someone in my peripheral vision approaching our table.

"Well, if this isn't our local famous author," came the feminine voice.

I glanced up to see a woman with red hair piled high on her head. She wore a low V-neck dress and stood so close to Grim that her hip was touching his shoulder.

He leaned away. *Good boy.* "Vanessa, nice to see you."

"It's very nice to see you," she said.

What was it with Grim? Did every woman who laid eyes on him just throw themselves at his feet? Like, what was the deal? If anything did happen between us, I'd be worried that some hussy would be waiting in the wings, ready to jump into his bed as soon as I was out.

"Vanessa, this is Paige Provey," Grim said.

Vanessa offered her hand. "The author. I know." She smiled like a snake, revealing pointy canines. Vampire. It was obvious.

I took her frigidly cold hand and gave it a slight shake. It took all my will not to shiver as our flesh touched.

"It's nice to meet you," I told her.

"Oh no, the pleasure is all mine. I am just delighted to finally get a chance to chat with you."

I prayed she wouldn't bring up what had gotten my career canceled —that Walter had declared on video that I was a fraud. You see, I used to (and still do) write paranormal books, and may have led readers on that I could see ghosts. That, of course, was before I could actually see spirits.

The thing was, in the past I never declared that I *couldn't* see ghosts. I never shouted from the rafters, *I can't see spirits.* But based on what I'd written, some readers inferred that I could communicate with the dead. Okay, I should have told them that I couldn't. I should have, when the rumors started to swirl, come out and declared that I could not, in any uncertain terms, talk to spirits.

But I never did.

It was such a rush, you see, having people fawn all over me, having them really look up to me as some sort of spiritual person. Yes, it was wrong to play into their beliefs. I'm not denying that. I'm only trying to explain *why* I let the rumors continue to swirl.

It was simply because it was easier to let them go on than it was to stop them.

So when my legion of fans discovered that I was nothing but a fraud, they turned on me, canceling me in an instant. I became nothing more than a gif or a momentarily relevant meme.

While I silently pondered what had brought me to Willow Lake, I prayed that Vanessa didn't bring any of that up.

Bless her if she didn't.

"Vanessa is head librarian at the Willow Lake Library," Grim told me.

"Oh, you are? Well, you know," I half joked, "I love to read."

"As do I," she murmured.

She leaned into me, and her lips pulled back into what a normal person would have considered a gruesome smile, given that she was a vampire and had all those pointy teeth and everything. But I was not a normal person. I was somewhere between a witch and a medium. I guessed that made me a *meditch* or a *wedium*.

She continued. "Tomorrow we're having a local author, Mitch Taylor, do a reading and signing for us. I would love it if you could come, maybe introduce him."

"Me? Oh, I wouldn't want to steal Mitch's thunder. That's his day." I also wasn't sure if I wanted to be seen in public by readers. There was no telling what they might throw at me in anger—cell phones, keys, wallets.

On second thought, I could have used any extra cash that floated my way. But before I could think of a means of explaining that, Vanessa cooed.

"Nonsense. You won't be stealing anything. Mitch knows that you're staying here for the summer, and he'd already said something to me about how wonderful it would be if you popped in."

Now I got it. Mitch wanted an *endorsement*. He thought that if I gave his book the Paige Provey seal of approval, then his sales would skyrocket.

Had he read the news lately? I was a social pariah.

But still, if I could get away from my sister for two hours, I considered that a bonus.

"Sure. I'll do it."

"Great." Vanessa smiled. "Let me give you the details."

When she was done writing everything down, I felt pretty good. Light, in fact. This could be good. It would be the start of me getting away from the old image of Paige Provey. It could be a new beginning— a fresh start.

Before Vanessa left, I said, "Tell me—what genre does Mitch write?"

Without missing a beat, Vanessa replied, "The occult."

Then she walked away. Well, there went me trying to get away from my old image. I'd walked right smack into it headfirst.

CHAPTER 3

*T*he rest of my evening with Grim was pleasant. He regaled me with stories of creatures that he'd hunted and captured, and he showed me a few of the battle scars to punctuate his point.

I traced my finger along a silvery scar about two inches long that was cut into his forearm. "And this one?"

"That was from a woodland sprite. It was about this big"—he parted his thumb and forefinger about two inches—"and had teeth twice that."

I laughed. "You're joking."

"Wish I was. That sprite bore down hard. He didn't stop biting until I pinched his head."

My hand flew to my mouth. "You didn't hurt it, did you?"

"Course not. I just let it know that I wasn't messing around. He let go and so did I."

I sank my elbow to the table and propped my chin in my hand. "What happened after that?"

"We parted ways and I hope never to see that creature again."

I laughed and so did he. We stared at each other for a long moment before Grim said, "Want to get out of here?"

God, yes. "Sure." No need to be overly exuberant. I might have been old enough that I no longer wanted to play games with the opposite sex, but there was no need for me to be so excited that Grim could smell my enthusiasm.

Being too enthusiastic for a man was never a good look. Even I knew that.

He wove through the back roads slowly. The moon was bright and white, and it made me wonder what the werewolves were doing. I hoped none of them were hiding in the woods, waiting to jump out and attack us.

To ease my worry, I tightened my hold around Grim's waist and pressed my head to his back. This was the life. Touching him, being so close felt right. It felt so good that I didn't want the evening to en—

We came to an abrupt stop, and my entire body crashed forward. "What happened?"

"Shh," was all he said. When a monster hunter told you to be quiet, you did so. Grim slowly dismounted. "Stay put," he said sternly.

That was never a good thing to hear. I had no problem being quiet, but I didn't want to be left alone, in the woods, by myself, when there was a full moon.

So I got off the bike and followed him. My foot landed on a twig and it snapped. Loud. Grim turned around.

"Stay," he snarled.

"I will not stay in some creepy woods at night by myself," I hissed. "No thank you. I will come with you and stay out of the way."

He looked at me and, after a long moment, grunted. "Fine. But no walking in front. If you do, the—"

I screamed as something jumped out of the bushes and attacked Grim. Grim roared as he was thrown across the forest floor and hit a tree.

I made out a hulking shape racing toward him. A light! I needed one so that I could see.

With trembling hands, I pulled up the flashlight on my phone and aimed it at the thing that looked like nothing more than a shadow.

Oh. My. Word.

The creature was easily seven, maybe eight feet tall with long tentacle arms, and it was covered in eyeballs.

My skin itched all over. Also, I felt the urge to puke at the same time. It was that grotesque.

Wait a minute. I'd seen it before. The thing was one of the creatures from the Heronomous What's-his-name book.

Grim had told me what it was called, but I couldn't remember. At that moment a name didn't matter because it was slowly making its way toward Grim, who was still groggy from colliding with the tree.

I grabbed the closest thing that I could find—a branch—and tossed it at the creature. "Hey, why don't you come over here and pick on me instead?"

The monster turned all its eyes toward me, and that itching sensation returned. But it apparently decided I wasn't enticing enough, and it continued approaching Grim.

This time I hurled a rock at it. "Hey, over here!"

The rock hit the creature in one of its dozen eyes. I vomited a little in my mouth. It pivoted its slimy arm-laden body in my direction and started toward me.

"Okay, Grim, you can wake up now. This thing's going to kill me."

"I told you to be quiet," he murmured.

I heaved another rock at the creature, but it didn't even flinch. "Grim! This thing's going to kill me."

Next thing I knew, the creature was flying in the opposite direction, into the trees and away from me. Grim stood where the thing had just been.

"I told you not to follow me," he scolded.

"And I told you that I wasn't going to be left alone."

"Now there's an *aghash* loose and it's mad."

That's what it was called. An aghash! "It's not my fault you got attacked."

Then Grim was on the ground and exhaling a shot of air. I aimed my light at him and saw that one of the tentacles was wrapped around his leg.

"Oh," he roared.

"What is it?"

"Poison," he said with a grunt.

"What can I do?"

"Stop talking," he told me.

Rude.

But before I could reply, Grim pointed a hand at the aghash and hit it with about a thousand volts of electricity. The squid-like creature shrieked and released Grim, who jumped onto his feet in a totally extreme Bruce Lee kind of way.

I didn't have time to be impressed because Grim moved in front of me. "Stay back," he spat before raising his hand again at the monster.

A thousand more volts of electricity went pulsing into the aghash, lighting up the night sky like fireworks. The creature contracted like jelly, and then it exploded everywhere.

I felt bits of things that I would rather not discuss land in my hair. I also felt something splat onto my chest and slither down my clothes.

"Are you okay?" Grim asked.

I was not okay. I was permanently scarred. "I'm fine," I squeaked out.

"Come on. Let's get to my house."

"Your house?"

"Unless you have a healing potion at your rental, one that will save my leg, yes, let's get to my house."

Okay, so his place it was. I offered my shoulder and helped him onto the bike. He got us to his house and made it to his door before he fainted just inside the threshold.

His winged dog, Savage, bounded up and started licking Grim's face. That seemed to wake him up.

"Where am I?"

"Let's get you up," I said.

I helped him onto his couch and pressed the back of my hand to his head. His skin was on fire. When I pushed up his pant leg, I saw why. There were oozing suction-cup-like marks on his flesh from the venom.

"Grim, wake up," I commanded. "I need help to find something that will save you."

"My workroom," he whispered.

I had no idea where that was, but that didn't stop me from charging into every closed door in the house. None of them had anything like a workroom.

Desperate, I spoke to Savage. "Where's Grim's workroom?"

The dog cocked his head before racing to the door that led to the greenhouse. Oh no. Inside there were all kinds of plants, but there were also creatures that Grim had collected. What if one of them tried to kill me?

Why would they kill me? Simply because I wasn't Grim and they were obviously crazy territorial like all wild creatures that existed?

Granted, I knew nothing of those creatures except what jumped from my overactive imagination, which was clearly a lot.

Going inside was a risk that I had to take. Hand trembling, I opened the door and flipped on the light, revealing a forest of plants and small trees. Potted greenery sat on counters that wound around the glass structure.

From the living room, Grim moaned. Okay, I needed to act and fast.

I followed Savage to the very back of the greenhouse where there was a small open space, almost like a classroom had been set up. There was a bench to one side and a table on the other. A bookcase lined one wall, and on it were rows upon rows of books.

Good grief, how would I find anything that could help in all that mess? I quickly scanned the titles and found one that was all about healing.

Jackpot!

I pulled it down and opened it on the table. The book slammed shut. I jumped back, shocked by what I'd seen.

Thinking that perhaps the binding was too tight, I opened the book again, and the same thing happened.

This tome had a mind of its own.

Well, so did I.

"Look," I said, "Grim has succumbed to venom. I need a potion that will help. Or something." The book was still for a moment, so I added, "Please."

It opened to a page with what looked like a recipe. I needed lemon peels, chamomile, and charcoal. Was I making tea? I studied it and glanced at another bookcase only a few feet away. I quickly located the charcoal and then raced into the kitchen, where I found a lemon and the tea.

I put the ingredients together, but it didn't look right. There wasn't a way to mix them. I spotted a mortar and pestle on the kitchen counter and started grinding the heck out of the trio. The juice from the lemon helped to create a paste. The paste I then took into the living room, where Grim was staring up at the ceiling, his eyes wild, sweat dripping down his forehead.

I didn't know if I could save him, but I had to give it my best shot. I put the mortar containing the paste down and ripped his jeans. Grim roared and thrashed.

"Stop it," I yelled. "You've got to stay put."

He mumbled something incoherent and settled down. I stared at the wounds and grimaced. They were pussed up and seeping. I prayed the paste worked. I slathered it on, and Grim screamed, I'm sure from the lemon juice. I wondered if the book was just screwing with me by showing me that healing serum.

I stared at the leg and waited for something to happen and then realized that there had been words with the paste.

"Be right back." I raced into the greenhouse, snatched the book from the table and ran it back toward the living room. When I reached the door, it felt like I hit a force field. The book flew from my hands, and I crashed to the floor. "What the…?"

I rose and grabbed the book again, racing toward the door, and when I reached the threshold, it flew from my hands again.

Magic, I realized, had been placed on the book to ensure it didn't leave the room. Which meant I would have to work the spell from the edge of the doorway.

Fine. Whatever. Anything to save Grim.

And that was when I realized that I was falling for him. My stomach folded over; my heart stuttered with fear at the very thought of him and that beautiful face of his losing all its life.

I would not let him die.

I began chanting, focusing on the words and hoping that even though I was several feet away, it would work.

Savage went over and lay down on the floor beside the couch, his head in his paws. He obviously sensed that something was wrong.

I'm trying to save your papa, I wanted to say.

The more I chanted, the less moaning Grim seemed to do. I stood for so long reciting the chant that I grew tired and had to sit. Eventually Grim went quiet.

Oh no. He was dead.

I had to check on him. After a few moments I found the courage to get up and cross to him.

Grim's face was coated in white salt from dried sweat. I sneaked a peek at his leg. The wounds were crusted over, and the redness and swelling were gone.

I placed the back of my hand to his forehead. The fever had broken, and he was resting comfortably.

I'd done it. I'd saved him. I slumped to the floor beside the couch, rested my arm on the lip of a cushion and dropped my head onto it. Exhausted, I closed my eyes and fell into a deep sleep.

CHAPTER 4

*W*hen I woke up, I found myself on the couch wrapped in a blanket. Sunlight streamed through the windows, and the scent of cooked sausage filled the room.

I stretched and blinked. How had I ended up here? Then I remembered—the aghash! And Grim had almost died.

I jumped from the couch and darted into the kitchen, where Grim stood at the stove. His leg was bandaged, and he was freshly showered and in new clothes.

Wish I could have said the same for myself—I was in a stained jumpsuit. There were probably leaves and debris in my hair, and even though I hadn't looked in a mirror, when I brushed a hand over my face, I'd felt something clinging to my skin. Dirt, I hoped.

"Morning," he said with a lopsided grin, not seeming to notice or care about my hideous appearance. "My memory is shoddy, but I think that I owe you my life."

"You don't remember anything?"

He plated a few sausage links and set them beside a bowl overflowing with scrambled eggs. "I remember you ignoring my command to *not* follow me."

"Right." My cheeks heated from embarrassment. "There was that."

"And I recall a certain aghash trying to kill me and shooting its venom into my leg."

"Hence the wounds. How do they look this morning?"

"I was going to let my nursemaid see to them."

"Oh, you have one of those? Where do you keep her, the closet?" I slapped my thigh in mock frustration. "Wish I'd known about her last night. It would have made healing you a lot easier."

Grim smirked. He motioned for me to sit at the small round table and I did so. Savage followed Grim like a shadow, his tongue out, saliva dripping to the floor. If he was like most dogs, he'd already eaten his first breakfast and was waiting impatiently for his second, human one.

I excused myself to the bathroom and washed up with towels that Grim had left for me. After rinsing my hair and face in the sink and wiping down my clothes, I felt clean enough to be presentable.

"Hungry?" he asked when I reappeared.

"I am. I guess sleeping on the floor will do that to a person."

He spooned a heaping amount of eggs onto my plate. "I moved you to the couch when I woke up."

"When was that? Oh, and can you pass the ketchup?"

He handed it to me, and I poured some on my hashbrowns. He had made hashbrowns and they looked perfect! Never in my life had I mastered perfect hashbrowns. The grated potatoes always stuck to the bottom of the frying pan, no matter how much oil I doused them with.

"Did you use magic to keep these from sticking?" I had to know his secret. "It's okay if you did. I won't tell anyone."

He shook his head. "No, my mother showed me how to cook them right."

"This mother of yours was quite the woman."

From what Grim had told me so far about her, she had been. She'd helped construct his greenhouse and apparently had magical powers akin to mine—she could take on the magic of someone she was near. I hoped that didn't mean Grim and I were related. Of course, even if we were, this was Alabama. It wasn't unknown for third cousins to have dated and married. We were like the royalty in that way. Yep, whenever I pictured royalty, thoughts of Alabama entered my mind.

Okay, they didn't.

I bit into the hashbrowns. They were perfect—crispy on the outside and soft on the inside. Cooked to perfection.

"I woke up in the middle of the night," he confessed. "You were asleep with your head propped on the couch. I placed you where I was and I got up and showered."

I wondered if he felt my fat rolls when he moved me. Not that I was like some huge beast or anything, but I had my tummy rolls like any middle-aged woman who wasn't Jennifer Aniston.

"Why'd you shower?"

"Whatever you did filled me with energy. I felt fantastic," he admitted.

Grim smiled, making the corners of his eyes crinkle. There was something charming yet intimate about the look, like the fanning at his eyes were a secret and he only let a few people see them.

Or perhaps that was simply those warm eyes of his. And this morning they overflowed with the stuff.

He cupped his hand over mine, and a stupid smile flitted on my mouth. We stared at each other, and a strange emotion sprouted like a seed in my chest, blooming all the way to my throat.

Grim was perfect. Yes, he was rough and mean and bossy and so, so alpha. But he was also warm and kind, gentle and caring. And I could fall for him.

The fact that he was easy on the eyes and a few years younger helped, too.

"So I found a book," I explained. "It was in your greenhouse." Which reminded me. "I couldn't leave the room with it, but I cooked up a poultice and then performed the chant from the edge of the greenhouse door. You were feverish and if I hadn't done something, you would have...well, it wouldn't have been good, let's just say. And I didn't know who to call."

His hand over mine squeezed. "You were amazing. I couldn't have asked for better treatment."

"Really?" I squeaked. *Why was I squeaking?* I cleared my throat and said much deeper, "Well, I'm just glad you're okay."

"If you get stuck with the venom of one aghash tentacle, you'll be very sick. But being stuck with as many as I was—it's usually deadly."

My stomach dropped. "Oh. Well, I'm glad that I found the right spell, then."

"Me too." He pulled his hand away and used it to hold his fork. Couldn't he try to eat left-handed, just for this meal? "But the greater concern is where the creature came from."

"What?" I joked. "You mean you don't have aghashes hanging out in the depths of Willow Lake?"

"No," Grim said grimly. Ha. Joke. "We don't, and I'm sure you're well aware of how it could've gotten here."

"The book," I murmured.

He nodded. "Exactly. I'm afraid that what we feared would happen is coming true."

"That whoever has the book with the creatures in it is unleashing them, one at a time, for some master plan?"

"Either that or they just want to toy with the town, release them slowly so that we know someone is in control, but not who."

"Sounds like some sort of sicko."

He grunted. "Wouldn't be the first time a sicko with magic decided to harm others."

A cold shiver worked its way down my spine. "What do we do?"

"Let the police know so that they can warn the community."

The officer in charge of Willow Lake was named Cowan. He was nice enough but not the sharpest tool in the shed. He had a penchant for becoming distracted in a conversation and talking about mundane things instead of what was really going on.

I could just imagine how he would explain about the book to the public. *Well, you see, there's this real dangerous book out there, like. Inside of it, there are all these creatures that can come out and turn real, harming you. Now, I know most of y'all would just call Grim if that happened. And I don't blame you. Who doesn't want a handsome man fighting a creature? He would be my first choice, too. But you see...*

And so on.

"I'll head to the police today," he said, breaking me from my thoughts.

"Let me know if there's anything that I can do to help."

"You can."

Oh? I hadn't expected him to actually take me up on my offer. He was the big, bad creature hunter, after all, and I was just the struggling writer. But why mince words?

"What do you need?"

He leaned over and kissed me, which surprised the heck out of me. My cheeks burned with heat. My…everything burned with super-charged hormonal attraction. He tasted of sausage and hashbrowns, and I was starving.

When he broke the kiss, Grim said, "I owe you another date. So you can go out with me."

"Yes," I managed, though my gut reaction was to say, *When? How? Now? In bed?* "I would like that."

"I hate that our date ended badly."

"It couldn't be helped."

"I know." Amusement flashed in his silvery eyes. "But I'd like to take you out again, tonight."

"Well, let me just check my calendar." I had nothing to check. I was free. But he could wait five minutes for that knowledge. "I'll let you know later."

He rose. "We should get you home."

"Why?"

Grim smirked. "Won't your sister be worried about you?"

Oh, right. Her. "She'll be fine." He shot me a skeptical look. "You're right. She's probably worried. I should get back."

I rose and he kissed me again. "Want to check my wound before you go?" he said in a husky voice.

"I would love to," I replied, breathless and dizzy from the kiss.

Grim sat and unwound the dressing from his leg. Oh, right. He'd *actually* been talking about the wound. I thought it was a euphemism for something else.

The punctures were crusted over nicely. All the red was gone from them, and they were healing beautifully.

I folded my arms and said proudly, "I should have been a doctor. I did a great job."

"You did. They barely even hurt. Just a bit tender, but that'll pass soon."

He closed the bandage and rose. "Ready?"

No. I wanted to stay all day. "Yep. Let's go."

~

"IT'S FINE. TOTALLY FINE," Cammie announced dramatically when I returned. "You can stay out all night and pretend that I didn't come to visit. I'm cool with that. Just let me know how the sex was. Don't leave out any of the dirty details."

I pointed to my smudged face and clothing. "Do I look like I spent all night making whoopee?"

"That's what I always look like the day after. So, yes."

What was my sister, a jungle monkey? Who spent the night with a man and returned looking like they'd been dragged down a dirt path?

Snow glanced up from the ghostly paper she was reading at the table. "All she complained about last night was that you were getting some and she wasn't."

I bit back a chuckle. Boy, I guessed Cammie was so jealous that she was talking to herself.

"So," Cammie said, "what're we gonna do today? Lay by the lake, get some sun? Or would you rather go shopping?"

"Neither."

"What? Why not?"

I brushed past her, heading for the shower. "I have an event at the library. There's a local author doing a signing, and I promised that I'd stop by."

"Well, I love the library. I would be pleased to go."

My expression fell. "Cammie, you and I both know you do not read books."

"I do, too. I read all kinds of books. I read one about this woman who had a harem that was all men, and then I read another one about this rich guy who liked to tie his girlfriend up and spank her."

Snow's brows rose to peaks. I had to shut Cammie up before she embarrassed *me*. She'd already done embarrassed herself. There was no saving her, but my reputation could still recover.

"Cammie, those aren't the types of books I'm talking about."

She scratched her chin in confusion. "I promise you that they were books." She hoisted her purse over her shoulder. "Besides, I came here to spend time with you. I'm not going to sit in a cabin all by myself while you're out and about."

Snow lifted her hand. "I would be here."

But to Cammie, she would still be alone. I sighed. "Fine. You can come. But just do me a favor and don't mention anything about the kinds of books you read—no reverse harems, no bondage. None of that. Do you understand?"

Her lips parted wide and she smiled. My sister looked truly happy, and a stab of sorrow pierced my heart. Who was I to dictate what she did? This could be good, me and Cammie spending time together.

"Oh, we're gonna have so much fun," Cammie gushed. "We're going to get the Southern back in you."

I paused. "What?"

"You know, the Southern."

"I have no idea what you're talking about."

Cammie clucked. "Paige, you and I both know that you've lost your Southern. You barely even have your accent anymore, and I didn't see one bag of cornmeal in your cupboard, or any frozen purple hull peas in the freezer."

"They don't sell purple hull peas in the grocery store."

"But they do at any farmer's market."

I scoffed. "I don't go to the farmer's markets."

"Exactly. Lost your Southern."

That was absurd. I was Southern. I hadn't lost touch with my roots, my heritage.

She hugged me tight. "Don't worry. We'll get it back in you. And after the library, we can go shopping. I can't wait to see what downtown Willow Lake has to offer."

Besides the vampires and werewolves, did she mean? She couldn't see them, of course. But if she could, my sister would be getting more than she bargained for when it came to Willow Lake.

Trust me.

CHAPTER 5

"Oh, what a cute little town," Cammie gushed as we entered the city limits. "I just love it here. I think I may get me a little apartment right here, so that I can grab a cup of coffee every morning."

Cammie was referring to Banshee's Beans, one of the coffee shops in town. Now, when I looked at the name, I saw one thing, but since Cammie didn't have magic, she should have read a different name.

To make sure of that, I tested her. "What name is on that placard?"

"Which one?" she asked, flinging dyed black hair over one shoulder.

"The coffee shop."

"You mean Beachnut Beans?"

"Right. Beachnut Beans. That's the name of it." I snapped my fingers as if the words had slipped my mind. "I forgot it."

Cammie tapped the glass. "How could you have forgotten it when it's staring you in the face?"

A trill of laughter erupted from my lips. "I don't know. I guess I'm just so sleepy."

"Must be from all that roughhousing you did last night. And I'm still miffed that you haven't given me any of the dirty details. That man's got a body on him. He is so fine." She shot me a contemptuous look. "I'm surprised you snatched him up."

"Excuse me, but he did ask me out."

"He's so much younger than you."

I grimaced. "Is it that obvious?" *Please don't let it be obvious.*

"Only to those of us who know that you're well into your forties. Anybody else might not guess. But I'm your sister and I know all." She patted my leg. "Don't you worry. I ain't gonna tell nobody. Your secret's safe with me."

I supposed that would have to do for now. But I wasn't exactly filled with a real sense of security knowing that my biggest secret could be unleashed from Cammie's mouth in the blink of an eye.

"Oh, look, we're here." I pulled into the library's parking lot, which was buzzing. There were lots of cars already taking up most of the spaces, leaving me to squeeze between a minivan and a tiny hatchback. "I think I got it."

"You got it. Just don't gain any weight while we're inside or we'll never squeeze back in."

She was joking. There was plenty of room to—

Oh, my door almost hit the minivan. The spot was tight, but there was room to make it work. I got out and smiled at Cammie, whose gaze zipped around. If I hadn't known any better, I would've thought that my sister was nervous.

"You ready?" I asked cheerfully.

"Sure. Let's go read some books."

"Well, we're not going to actually read any. I'm going to introduce the main guy and tell them how much I love his work."

Her expression fell. "Oh. So you're going to lie."

"I'm not going to lie. I'm just going to stretch the truth."

We headed toward the front door. "Have you ever even read any of his work?"

"Well, um, no. But that's not the point. The point is—"

"You're going to lie."

"Yes, I suppose so." I grabbed the door and opened it, letting Cammie go inside first. "Let's just keep that between the two of us."

Vanessa greeted me almost immediately. "Paige, thank you for coming."

"I wouldn't have missed it for the world." I pointed to Cammie. "This is my sister, Cammie. Cammie, this is Vanessa, she's the head librarian."

"Oh, good. Maybe you can point out where to find the *Kama Sutra* books."

Vanessa's eyes bulged. "The what? I'm sorry?"

I swatted Cammie's arm none too playfully. "She's kidding." I gave my sister a sharp look, one that said, *Do not embarrass me.* "So. Where's Mitch? I'm dying to meet him."

"He's just over here." Vanessa walked us to a ring of three people talking—one man with his back to me wearing a blazer, a short woman with wide hips wearing a floral dress, and an older gentleman who had the college professor air about him. "Mitch?"

The man with his back to me turned, and I was presented with Mitch Taylor. He had short dark hair, wire-rimmed glasses, bright brown eyes and a cherubic face. Why, he didn't look much older than twenty, but I sensed that was more about the fact that he had a baby face than his actual age.

He excused himself from the two people that he'd been talking to. "Yes?"

Vanessa linked her cold, fish-fleshy-feeling arm through mine. "This is Paige Provey and her sister, Cammie."

"Paige, I'm delighted to meet you." He clasped my hands. "When Vanessa told me that you were staying in town, I dared to hope that you might, just might come and visit with our little book signing. Thank you so much."

"Of course. I'm always happy to support another writer."

Vanessa tapped her watch. "You have a few minutes to chat before we get started. I've got some things to attend to, so please excuse me."

"Of course," I said. "Do what you need to do." When Vanessa disappeared, I spotted a mountain of books on a table and pointed to them. "Oh, is that your latest?"

"Yes, it sure is. This one was a labor of love. Took me over two years to write."

Cammie grabbed a cheese and cracker from a nearby tray and stuffed it into her mouth. "Look, Paige, now you can read one of his books." She leaned over toward Mitch. "She hasn't read nothing that you've written before, but I told her that she had to after this. You got any steamy love scenes in your books? I love a good steamy love scene—one that describes a man's chest and tight buttocks. Those are my favorite."

Mitch's face paled. I gently pushed Cammie toward the sea of people waiting to hear Mitch speak. "Why don't you go find a book? Check that aisle over there."

"But those are kids' books."

"Great place to start." I turned my back to her, hoping Cammie would get the hint and leave us alone—forever.

"So." I smiled, hoping to erase any negative taste that Cammie might have left in Mitch's mouth. "Tell me about your new book."

"Well," he said, placing a hand to his heart, "it's about a group of teenagers who stumble onto a sacrificial stone while they're at summer camp."

"Oh?"

"And then the murders begin."

I laughed, thinking that Mitch was joking. When he didn't begin chuckling, I quickly backpedaled. "Sorry. It was just that sounded like that game that people play where they read the first sentence of a book and then for the second one, you say, 'and then the murders began.'" I paused. "But that wasn't what you meant, was it?"

"No." He grinned. Apparently I hadn't offended him. "It's not the game. But this book is about ancient magic, evil, all the sort of stuff that teenagers love."

I glanced over his shoulder and then noticed that much of his audience was teens. I spotted a girl in a ponytail and short skirt, a nerdy boy in a loose-fitting T-shirt and a jock standing in the corner, looking like he didn't want to be anywhere near the reading.

I pointed to them as well as to the adults. "Looks like your books pull in quite a range of folks."

He smiled proudly. "Yes, scholars and academics are interested in this book, too."

My brows shot up. "Scholars? Are you sure that I should be here, introducing you?"

He laughed and lightly touched my arm. Was he flirting? "Of course

29

you should be. I'm honored that you'd come. But as to the academics, they're here because of what's *in* my book."

"What's that?"

Mitch grabbed a copy off the stack and opened it. It was in hardcover, and he was careful not to crack the binding as he leafed through the pages, locating the one he searched for.

"Here it is. Take a look."

I spotted a series of lines that looked like poetry.

Evil, evil, reigns the day, bring me shame, come what may. To this all I ask of you, come into my life, tried and true.

The text went on, but I didn't read it all, only those couple of lines. "Ah, that's some good poetry."

"It's more than poetry." Mitch's voice dropped. "When I was doing my research, I located several places where rituals had been performed. And in one of those, I found this text."

"What is it?"

"The best that I can gather is that it's some occult ritual, a spell written before a sacrifice occurred."

I shivered. "That's creepy."

"And that's why the scholars are interested in it. No one had found the spot before. I had to search far and wide, talk to locals about places rumored to be where animal sacrifice had occurred in order to even find the location." He closed the book and held it proudly to his chest. "So you see why this was a labor of love."

"Definitely. A lot of research went into it."

He placed the book down. "So. Are you working on something new?"

"Yes, I am. It's a little different than my other books, but still in the same vein."

Which reminded me, I needed to get pages to Madeleine, my literary agent. She'd been hounding me for them. I still had another two months before the book was due. I'd just hit a wall, was all, and I wasn't ready to tell my agent about it yet.

In the past, whenever I'd had writer's block, I always found a way around it. But at the moment the words weren't coming. They would, though. I had faith.

"I said, I had that book first. Let it go!"

Cammie's voice rang out through the crowd. What in the world? She'd had one job—*one!* All she had to do was find a book and quietly read it.

"You snatched it from my hand," came another voice.

"Would you excuse me?" I left Mitch and headed in the direction of the voices. I found Cammie and the woman wearing the floral dress both in the romance aisle. "What is going on?"

The woman pointed to Cammie. "This woman here snatched this book right out of my hand."

Cammie shrugged. "I thought that she was done with it."

The woman's jaw fell. "How can I be done with it when I'm still holding it?"

"I thought your fat fingers had slipped off it," Cammie accused.

I wanted to die.

"How dare you call me fat," the woman said. "No one calls Lulu Stiles fat."

"I think I just did," Cammie said.

"Well, you're a box-dyed brunette!"

"My hair is ebony, thank you very much." Cammie hugged her arms to her chest. "And I didn't want that old book anyway."

"Good. Because the way you're acting, you would only get it over my dead body!"

Everyone in the library was watching us. Okay, it might not have been everyone, but it certainly felt like it.

"Fine." Cammie exhaled hard. "Here. Take the book. The man on the cover doesn't look hot anyway. I'll find another one to read."

With that, Cammie charged off. I turned to Lulu. "I'm so, so sorry. She's going through a rough time."

Not at all, but it couldn't hurt to say that.

Lulu huffed and pulled her purse up higher on her shoulder. "Well, she should learn some manners."

"I agree." Then I smiled. "Listen, let's go find you a seat because I have a feeling that the reading is about to take place."

Just then, Vanessa strode up to the microphone and started talking. I wheeled Lulu to the chairs and prepared to speak.

CHAPTER 6

"Good morning, everyone," I said.

"Good morning," they replied back.

Okay, what was I supposed to do next? Oh, right. Introduce Mitch. "My name is Paige Provey, and when I was asked to introduce Mitch Taylor, I said that I would be honored. Ever since I read his first book, I was hooked. I was drawn into his world and with his newest book"—I leaned over to catch the name of it—"*Slasher of Sacrifice*"—oh, God, was that really the title?—"I know that I'll be drawn into a wonderful world full of…" Here I faltered. A world full of sacrifice? The occult? Then it hit me. "A world full of complex characters and a well-written plot." Time to get off the stage before someone asked me details about a Mitch Taylor book. "Everyone, let's give a warm welcome for Mitch."

Everyone clapped, me included, and I welcomed him and then stepped aside so that he could give his reading. I spotted Cammie in the back and darted over to her.

Her nose was buried in a book. She wasn't fooling anybody. My sister didn't read. She watched television. She sunbathed. She did not crack paper spines and peruse novels.

"Just what were you doing earlier, getting into that fight?" I snapped.

"I don't know what you're talking about."

I glared at her. "You do, too. We're just here to have a nice time, smile at a few people and then leave."

Cammie dropped the book to her side. "For your information, that fat woman started everything."

"And how did she do that?"

"She took one look at me in the aisle and scoffed, made this throat-clearing sound and said real low, like she thought I was deaf, 'Well, takes all kinds in here now, doesn't it?'"

My jaw unhinged and nearly fell to the floor. "You're joking."

"I am not joking," she said smugly. "She accosted me first. I was just defending myself." My sister stopped and stared at me. "If you ever really looked at me, you might know that."

I laughed nervously. "I really look at you. Of course I do."

Cammie smirked. "Sure you do."

"I do. You're my sister."

"Okay, then. What do I like to do for fun?"

"Well, um, you like to sit on the beach and get tan. You obviously like to dye your hair dark colors."

She shook her head. "Those aren't my hobbies."

"Fine," I bit back. "What is it that you like to do, Cammie? What have I been missing?"

She smiled, her lips parting wide with pleasure. "I like to play poker. I also like to sip lemonade and watch the sunset."

"I don't want your Tinder profile."

"That's what I like. I also enjoy romance novels—and some mysteries. I like your books."

She'd read my stuff? My sister read books? Not just the daily horoscope? "You do? You like my work?"

"I love your books. I've been dying for the latest one to come out."

"You have?" I was so touched. Sure, I sent her a copy of my latest whenever it released, but I didn't think that she really read them. I figured my books just went on a dusty shelf so that she could bring them down and show her friends. "I never knew that."

She gave me the side-eye. "Guess there's a lot of stuff that you don't know about me."

I supposed there was. Wow. How had I been so cut off from my sister? So oblivious?

We'd grown apart over the years as people do, and there was a big enough age gap between us that we each just allowed the distance to grow. We'd never been super close as kids. I was always too little to play with her and her friends, and she was simply never interested in me. As soon as she was eighteen, she was out of the house, living her messy life full of boyfriends and low-wage jobs until she got her cosmetology license.

I was working through high school, trying to earn enough money for a college degree that I never used. Then I married and sold my first book. Then I sold my second, and the rest was history.

But all that time, while I'd been busy writing and enjoying my big house and sleek cars, Cammie had been quietly cutting hair, marrying and divorcing husbands. The only time we'd see one another was at Christmas, when we all got together and spent an awkward afternoon catching up and pretending like we understood how the other half lived.

I'd never understood Cammie, but perhaps it was time that I did. I wasn't getting any younger and neither was she. At some point something would happen and one of us wouldn't be around. I didn't want to regret anything, especially since we actually had time to get to know one another right now.

So instead of seeing her presence as a thorn in my side, it was time that perhaps I started seeing it as a blessing.

From behind the lectern, Mitch Taylor finished his reading and the library erupted into applause. Jerked from my reverie, I started clapping and realized that I'd lost sight of Cammie.

"Mitch will be signing books now," Vanessa announced. "You can purchase his latest from me. I've got a whole stack over here." She patted the books and smiled. "A big thank-you to everyone who came."

People made their way to the front of the room, and I held back, waiting to congratulate Mitch until the crowd thinned out.

I did catch sight of Cammie, who was perusing the romance shelves again. Wow. She really did have a hankering for a good romance. Would wonders never cease?

"Thank you for coming," Vanessa said when I made my way to her.

"You're very welcome. I don't know if my presence helped, but I certainly hope so."

She smiled, which showed off her pointy canines. I'd hate to be on the receiving end of those. Ouch. "Your presence was definitely noticed. I think you have a few admirers."

When she said that, I spotted a couple of readers huddled together, shyly glancing at me. I smiled and the women smiled back.

"Mitch has quite a following, too," I told her.

"It's no wonder with how authentic his books are. They take years of research to write, and people love that. He makes the words jump off the page."

"Well, I'm sold. I'll be buying a copy."

She smiled. "Wonderful. Talk to you soon."

"Sounds good." Vanessa moved away and I joined the line, holding the copy of *Slasher of Sacrifice* Mitch had handed me earlier. After a few minutes, I reached him. "Hey, there. I enjoyed your talk."

"You did?" He beamed. "That means a lot coming from you."

"Oh, stop it. We're both authors here."

He smiled and pointed to the book in my hands. "Would you like it signed?"

"Well, I think that I have to pay for it first. Where'd Vanessa go?" I glanced around but didn't spy her. "She must've dashed off."

"Don't worry. I already bought all the copies. This one's on me. For coming today."

I eyed him skeptically. "You sure?"

"Absolutely." He grasped the book and opened the front cover. "To Paige, for helping me out."

"Thank you," I said with sincerity.

"No problem." Mitch glanced around me. "Well, I guess you were the last person here. Looks like my time's up."

"It was nice meeting you," I said.

We said goodbye and I turned but didn't see my sister. Now where had Cammie gone? I stalked around the library and, after some time, finally located her in the children's section. She was sitting on a stuffed elephant and had a sucker in her mouth.

"What are you doing over here?" I demanded.

"Being in my happy place. No one's talking over here, and they even have candy." She pointed to a bowl sitting atop a vacant librarian's desk. "You should get one."

"I don't want one." Then I thought better of it. "Do they have root beer flavor?"

She pulled a sucker from her pocket. "Sure do."

I snatched it and unwrapped the candy. "Thanks. Now, come on. Let's get out of here."

We reached the house, and Cammie plopped onto my one sofa soon as we entered, books in hand. She'd checked a couple out from the library. Actually I hadn't seen her talk to a librarian, but she claimed to have checked them out.

Somehow I got the feeling that my sister had simply snatched them from the facility. Who snatched books from a community library? Didn't matter. I'd make sure that they got returned.

I placed *Slasher of Sacrifice* on a small table beside the couch, and Cammie picked it up. "This looks interesting."

"Does it? It's got quite the title."

Cammie laughed. "Yeah, not what I usually read, but I could make an exception. Maybe it's like the *Friday the 13th* movies and has a little bit of everything—romance, horror, all that good stuff."

I rolled my eyes. "Yeah. All that good stuff."

Cammie thumbed through the book before laying it on the table. "So. What do you want to do this afternoon? Hit the lake's beach and soak up some rays? Go cruising in your car?"

"With gas prices where they are now? I'm definitely not up for wasting fuel."

Her expression fell. "Oh. Well, I'd like to do something. I ain't gonna be here too long."

My phone bleeped. In came a text from Grim asking if we were still on for that night. I replied that we were. "Look, I'm sorry to do this to you, but I've got another date."

"A date?" Her brows shot up. "With that guy? Again? You two had a lot of fun, didn't you? You just cain't say no to him, huh?"

"Let's just say things didn't go as expected."

"You didn't come back until this morning. How could they not have gone well?"

I wasn't about to explain about the aghash. "They just didn't, okay? So he's making it up to me."

"Mm hm." Cammie rose and stretched. Her short shirt rode up, revealing her abs. How old was she, again? "Well, I ain't gonna stick around here. If you're going out, I am too."

"You can't go out."

"And why not?" She folded her arms. "Tell me why I cain't."

I couldn't explain about the creature, and that there were lots of other creatures in the magic book, so I just said, "Um, just make sure you don't go for any walks alone. In the dark. Drive everywhere."

She stared at me for a long minute before saying, "Fine. Now. What have you got in your closet that I can wear?"

Yep. She was the same old Cammie. I wondered if I could convince her to wear something demure. Like a normal-length blouse and jeans?

CHAPTER 7

*T*urned out, I could not. Cammie found the smallest shirt in my closet and paired it with my tightest jeans. I had a feeling that she did so just for spite.

So while she was putting on makeup and slipping on a pair of my stilettos, I was shimmying into a light summer dress.

"You look nice," Cammie said, eyeing my top.

"You could have worn it." I turned my back toward her. "Can you zip me up?"

"Sure."

"Thanks."

After she did so, I turned to face her. "How do I look?"

"Almost as good as the time that you fell into a patch of poison ivy."

I swatted her shoulder playfully. "Oh yeah? Well, you look about as good as a…" *Hooker on the lot of the Flying J gas station* did not seem an appropriate reply. "You look nice, too. I know a great place for you to eat at tonight. There's a bar and steak house downtown and the bartender's awesome. His name's Ferguson and he's a lepre—"

I stopped before I could blurt out that Ferguson was a leprechaun. I could not, under any circumstances, explain to my sister about that. First of all, she wouldn't believe me. Secondly, she would have me committed.

"He's what?" she asked, face all twisted in question.

"He's one lucky devil. Yeah, good luck follows wherever he goes."

"Oh, okay." She ran a brush through her hair. "For a second there I thought that you were going to say that he's a leprechaun."

"A leprechaun? No. I would never say that." I shot her a look that suggested she'd gone crazy. "There's no such thing as leprechauns."

She laughed, too. "I know. That's why it would have been wackadoodle for you to talk about one."

Just then, the doorbell rang. Saved by the bell. "That must be Grim. I'll be right back."

"So, is that his first name or what?"

"Um, his last name?" To be honest, I didn't know. Since we were dating, perhaps I should have found out personal things about him. "Yes, his last name."

"Huh. Funny."

I opened the door, fully expecting to see a hunky man behind it, and was surprised when I came face-to-face with Patricia, my landlady.

She wore capri pants, sneakers and a bright floral Hawaiian-style T-shirt. "Hey, Paige, how're you? Everything good?"

"Um, yes. Everything's great." It was late. Why was she here? "Is everything okay with you?"

"Yes, yes, great. Just wonderful. As you can see"—she pointed to her shirt—"I'm about to go out of town for a few days."

"Right."

"And I wanted to let you know that if anything breaks, you can call my nephew, here." She stepped to the right, revealing a tiny human, around eleven or twelve years old. "This here is Abe, short for Abraham. He'll be helping while I'm gone, looking in at all my properties, making sure everyone's doing the right thing."

She lifted a brow suspiciously, as if I was about to throw a fraternity party in my one-bedroom cabin. I smiled at Abe. "Well, hello there. What sort of things can I call you about?"

He puffed out his chest. He was so cute with his light brown skin and curly brown hair. He also had bright blue eyes and a smile full of straight teeth.

"Well, ma'am," he said in a thick drawl, "you can call me if you need just about anything. My aunt gave me a cell phone, so if you get a hankering for ice cream or a cheeseburger, I can run it out to you—for a delivery fee, of course."

I bit back a laugh. He was just so darned cute. "Well, I have a car, but if I need anything delivered, I will call you. But you don't look old enough to drive, so how do you deliver things?"

He smiled proudly. "On my bike. It's got a rack for carrying food and other goods."

"That's very smart."

"Thank you."

Patricia placed a hand on Abe's shoulder and smiled at him warmly. "Yep, Abe here is a great help. Sorry that I haven't brought him by earlier; I've just been bogged down with life." She inhaled deeply. "Yep. That's why I'm going on vacation."

"Oh, I completely understand." I took Abe's hand and shook it. "Well, I will be glad to have you look in on me while your aunt's away." To Patricia I said, "How long will you be gone?"

"At least a week, but if I fall in love with the place, I might stay longer." She leaned forward and whispered, "I'm going to meet my sweetie out there. We've been Internet buddies for a while, and we're going to see if it's the real thing."

"That's wonderful," I gushed. "I hope it all works out for you."

"Me too. But in the meantime, you've got Abe here. If something breaks, call him. He knows who to have fix everything."

Impressive. He was very young for that kind of responsibility. "Will do."

They said goodbye and I disappeared back into the cabin. I had just slipped on my shoes when the bell rang for the second time.

Grim had arrived. I said goodbye to Cammie, told her to have a great night, and I stepped out to enjoy some time with Grim.

"How're you feeling?" I asked.

"Healed." He flexed his knee. "You made all the difference, and you're still learning your magic."

"That's the best part," I said proudly.

There was a basket strapped to the rear of his bike. "What's all this?"

He brushed his fingers down my arm, sending goose bumps spraying across my skin. "It's for a picnic on the lake."

He helped me get on the back of his bike, which was awkward wearing a dress. But I managed to tuck the fabric down in all the right places. I was getting too old to be hiking my leg to get on a vehicle, but there was something thrilling about all of it.

My ex-husband, Willard, hadn't had one bone of fun in his entire body. He'd been about being careful, cautious. I'd spent years making sure that I did things like rinsed out the tuna can after emptying the fish into a bowl because the smell grated on Willard's nerves. He was picky like that about everything.

And to be honest, I had gotten so used to it that to be with a man who did things like capture dangerous creatures and ride a motorcycle was thrilling.

"Let me see if I understand your plan," I said, almost teasing. "We're going to have a picnic and hope no aghashes show up."

"That's it." He smiled briefly before turning his back to me and sliding onto the bike. "I told Cowan about it, just so the police know."

"What are they going to do?" I asked.

"Since it was a one-time incident, nothing."

Nothing? What if someone else got hurt? What if another aghash was released from the book? Was doing nothing really the best way for the police to go about keeping the public safe?

But before I could argue, Grim started the bike and we flew off down the road headed toward the lake.

THE CRYSTALLINE WATERS were splendid to behold. The surface shimmered like a thousand diamonds had been scattered atop it. In the distance, past the tall pines, the sky was smeared with pinks and blues as the day birthed the coming night.

I lay back on the big checkered blanket that Grim had brought, and sighed. "How many stars will we see once the sky becomes black?"

"Too many to count." He lifted a champagne bottle. "More?"

I waved my hand. I'd already had two glasses and was feeling heady. "No thanks." He stretched out beside me, leaning his arm against the ground. I studied him. "You don't look like much of a lounger."

He frowned, confused. "Lounger?"

I sat up and a flash of disappointment flickered in his eyes. "You know, how you're lying now, with your legs out."

He glanced down at his posture. "Am I not supposed to lie this way?"

"No, no. It's just…you're a monster hunter. You seem more like the type who stands and broods rather than reclines and ponders."

"I assure you, I ponder."

This I found amusing. "Like what?"

"Like this."

He slid his hand behind my head and pulled me forward into a kiss. I moaned. Actually moaned. I hadn't moaned during a kiss since Walter and I had first gotten together. In the beginning, believe it or not, there had been a mountain of passion between us. That was what I felt now—singular rising passion that burned deep in my core.

Then my hands were acting on their own as I buried them in his mane of hair. Grim smelled musky and I drank in his scent. It filled me all the way to my toes, and they curled. Not a comfortable position as they were shoved into sandals.

Then I was on my back and we were kissing more and more, and it was all so romantic with the lake and the sunset and the boat motor running in the distance.

Wait. Boat motor?

I wiggled out from under him and sat up. Out on the waters were a bunch of teenagers guzzling beer and shouting on a boat.

"Interrupted by others with raging hormones," Grim grouched.

"So we are." With the mood broken, I changed the subject. "Going back to the aghash."

He sat up, a much more appropriate position for a monster hunter. "What about it?"

"Do you think people should know to be on the lookout for creatures?"

He nodded.

"But the police don't."

His lip turned up in one corner. "You think I should sound the alarm bell? Hold a meeting and inform the people?"

"Yes."

He dragged his gaze from me and studied the water, where the teenagers on the boat were slowly turning away and heading back in the direction that they'd come in.

"And what if I told you that I'd already sounded the alarm?"

"You mean, you're letting people know that they should be on alert?"

He nodded, didn't say anything.

"Then I'd say that sounds like the right call. It's what needs to happen. We don't know what all is in that book."

"That's what I told him."

I frowned. "Who? Cowan?"

"No. Ferguson."

"Why'd you tell Ferguson?"

Grim's piercing gaze slid back to me, sending a shiver radiating down my spine. "Because he's mayor of the witches and wizards in this town, and if someone needed to know, it's him. Come on."

He rose and offered his hand. "Where are we going?" I hoped our date wasn't over yet.

"To the steak house."

"Why?"

He smiled, which made my knees knock together. "For a drink. Why else?"

CHAPTER 8

The steak house was hopping when we arrived. People milled by the bar in clumps and swatches. Women wore glittery dresses and men wore suits.

I glanced down at my own clothing and shrank. "I feel underdressed."

Grim took my hand and squeezed with encouragement. "Don't. This is a private party."

"Yeah, the kind that's a lot fancier than how I'm dressed."

He stopped crossing the dining room and faced me. The force of his movement, the strong line of his jaw made me suck in a breath like I was holding it in order to shimmy into a tight dress. Or corset. Well, since this wasn't the eighteen hundreds, I supposed a dress would suffice for our purposes.

He stared down at me with such intensity that I thought his gaze would bore a hole straight through me. Totally and completely uncomfortable, I slapped a hair from my face and wound up slapping my nose.

"Ouch!"

"Are you okay?" He reached for my face. "Are you all right?"

I burned with embarrassment. "Yes, I'm totally fine. I go around slapping myself all the time."

My hands were touching my nose, and Grim took them gently. "Let me see. Make sure you didn't bruise anything."

"Other than my ego?" A few people glanced at me after having witnessed the slap heard round the world.

"Oh no, it looks like you broke it."

Had I? Had I actually managed to break my nose? Surely not. "What? Are you joking?"

He smiled, making the corners of his eyes crinkle in amusement. "Yes, I'm kidding. Come on. Let's wade through this party and talk to Ferguson."

We pushed our way to the bar and found Ferguson busy pulling taps and shaking martinis.

"Fergie," Grim said warmly. "Looks like quite the party."

The bartender handed a man his change and made his way over to us. "Some kind of launch party for a book."

My eyebrows peaked at that. "Oh? *Slasher of Sacrifice?*"

He rubbed his chin. "I'm not sure. All I know is that it's a local author."

"That's the one," came an incredibly familiar voice. I didn't want to look and see the body that the voice was attached to, but I forced myself to anyway. When my gaze landed on a stool at the corner of the bar, Cammie patted the seat beside her. "Fancy running into y'all two tonight. Come on and cop a squat right here. Two suits just left. They're nice and warm."

Grim nodded. "Thank you."

He took a spot two stools from my sister, leaving me the empty one beside her. "So. What've you been up to all evening?" I asked.

"I've been up to getting to know this man." Cammie grinned as Fergie crossed back to us. "We've been having a great time, haven't we?"

Fergie glanced up from the pint glass he was washing and smiled. The rosy color of his cheeks popped against his pale skin.

Oh. My. God.

My sister and the leprechaun were getting friendly. What was this world coming to? She tipped her face up to him and smiled. He grinned back, all toothy and smitten-like.

I couldn't let my sister lure the leprechaun into her arms so that she could suck him dry like a black widow and leave him abandoned after she'd taken all the love he had to give.

Not that I knew for certain that would happen, but let's just say that Cammie's track record with men was less than stellar—for *them*. She was an expert at ripping out hearts and eating them for breakfast.

Trying not to retch at the look of desire she shot Ferguson, I patted her arm and said in my most dissuading voice, "You won't be staying here long enough to fall for anyone."

She sighed hopelessly. "I already have. What a man he is."

If she saw his stilts, she'd agree—*what a man*.

Grim ordered a couple of drinks for us, and when Ferguson delivered them, he said, "We need to talk farther about the situation."

Ferguson's bushy brows lifted. "Tell me more."

"People need to know." Grim ran a finger along the glass in front of him. "I'm afraid the situation could get out of control."

"Are there more?" Ferguson asked.

Just as Grim started to answer, Cammie spoke. "So. What've you two lovebirds been up to tonight?"

I sighed, reluctant to drag my attention from the men. "We had dinner by the lake."

Cammie leaned back and got a good look at Grim. "I bet that's not all you did."

Could she stop embarrassing me? "It is. Cammie, I wish you would lay off the innuendos in front of Grim. It's really getting on my nerves."

She frowned. "Oh, you know I'm just playing, don't you?"

"Yeah, but adults don't play like that."

"Who said I'm an adult?"

"Good point."

My sister lifted her wineglass and took a small sip of the burgundy inside. That was the only wine she drank—burgundy. She said that all other varieties gave her a headache.

She settled the glass back down and nudged me with her elbow. "I'm just teasing you, sis. It just looks like you got a good man, there, is all."

A dark expression flashed across her face and my jaw dropped. "Why, Cammie, are you jealous?"

She threw back her head and laughed. "Course not. I ain't jealous of anyone except Pamela Anderson, and that was only in the nineties because she was built the way that I wanted to be—all boobs and tiny waist."

It was my turn to laugh. "You have nothing to be jealous of. I'm a mess. I can't write. Hit a rough patch and can't figure it out. I'm also living in a rented cabin with a lease that's up in a couple of months. Where am I going after that? No clue. Oh, and also I see ghosts."

Oh crap. I wasn't supposed to have said that.

Cammie did a double take. "You what?"

"I see ghosts of boyfriends past." Not knowing what else to do, I jerked my head toward Grim, who at that point was deep in conversation with Ferguson. "You know, it's hard to be in a new relationship when the old one went so sour, so badly."

Cammie eyed Grim hungrily, like he was a steak right off the grill. "I don't know how anyone could think of an old relationship with him warming their bed."

"Well, there hasn't been any of that. I'm obviously too wounded."

Her mouth pinched in confusion. "From Walter? You ain't wounded from him, are you?"

I was digging myself a hole that I'd never climb out of. "Yes, from Walter. I loved him for so long. He wasn't all bad in the beginning, you know."

She scoffed. "Yeah, he sure did pull the wool over your eyes. I took one look at him and knew that he was no good. I tried to tell you, but you wouldn't listen."

"Was that before or after you'd divorced Eric for gambling away all your money?"

Cammie lifted her glass and saluted the air. "See? I could tell Walter was no good because I'd been living with *no good* myself. I had a front-row seat."

"Oh please, Cammie. You didn't want me to be happy because you weren't. It was just like high school. You were happy to throw me under the bus about all those prom dresses, and were happy once again to make sure my life was full of misery, which was why you told me not to marry Walter."

She straightened and studied me. "Is that what you really think? That I said you shouldn't marry him because I didn't want you to be happy?"

"Isn't it obvious? That's how it always was between us. You had to have the last word on everything, be in charge of it all. If the narrative of the day didn't fit into your world, you changed the narrative."

She grasped my hand with such ferocity I startled. "Paige, I have only ever wanted what's best for you."

"Yeah, right."

"I hav—" Cammie dropped my hand as quickly as she'd grabbed it. Her gaze darted to the side and she stiffened.

I turned around, trying to see what had startled her. The door to the steak house was shutting, and a man with dark hair stood in front of it. He scanned the room and smiled at a woman in a yellow summer dress, who greeted him with a kiss to his cheek.

"What is it?" I asked my sister.

She stared for another moment before blinking. "Nothing. But anyway, I'm sorry that you felt like that. I never wanted you to. But I was in my own world all the time. It was hard being the older sister. There was a lot of pressure to guide you, and I wasn't always great at it." She laughed bitterly. "Like with that whole prom dress fiasco. But if I'd told my friends what had really happened, they would never have forgiven me. They would've thought I ruined their dresses on purpose. I was on thin ice with them anyway over some stupid disagreement. If they had known the truth"—she sighed sadly—"they would've pulled a prank in front of the entire school, something to humiliate me. That's why I did it, Paige, why I told them it was your fault instead of mine for what happened. They didn't do nothing to you, they just assumed it was an accident. But if they'd known the truth, they would have ruined me."

Was that a tear in the corner of my eye? I blinked it out and swiped it away with my fingers before she could notice.

I'd always assumed my sister was out to take care of herself, not caring about anyone else. High school friendships could be toxic. The bullying could crush a person's soul.

"I couldn't tell you," she admitted, her eyes brimming with sadness, "because being three years older than you, at least back then, it felt like a lifetime. I was all alone. Couldn't ask anyone for help."

Our mom had worked two jobs and only sat down to dinner with us once a week. We were thrown into the world to take care of ourselves. It broke my heart that Cammie had felt so alone and that for years I'd held her responsible for my own misery, when all our tender feelings could've been eliminated with this simple conversation.

I squeezed her shoulder. "I'm so sorry that happ—"

"All I wanted was for you to sign my book!"

The woman yelling was so loud that every conversation in the room came to a halt. I turned around and spotted Lulu from the library. She stood in front of Mitch, waving a copy of *Slasher of Sacrifice*. Her face was bloated with anger, and her legs were splayed wide. Mitch looked completely taken aback, like she'd just poofed out of nowhere demanding his John Hancock.

She shoved the hardback in his face. "You said that you'd sign my book! Now I want it signed. Or else you're going to regret it!"

CHAPTER 9

*G*rim glanced over his shoulder at me. "Do I have to get involved?"

"No, of course not," I said sarcastically. "Why would a heaping god of a man like yourself get involved when the room is full of what looks like a Geek Squad convention?"

He rolled his eyes because what I said was true. Though the restaurant was filled to capacity, all the bodies taking up the space were nerds who looked like they holed themselves in their parent's basements every Saturday to play Dungeons & Dragons old school.

As Grim lumbered from his stool, Ferguson threw him a word of warning. "Watch out for a woman scorned."

"Scorned out of getting her book signed," Grim said with a snort.

Lulu, meanwhile, had not stopped berating Mitch, who glanced nervously around at all the folks gathered to celebrate him.

He tugged on his shirt collar. "Sure, sure. I'll sign it."

"You said that you'd sign it in blood," Lulu said.

And just when I'd thought the room couldn't get any stiller, it became soundless, like a vacuum in space.

Grim reached her and said quietly, "Ma'am, I think you should go."

Lulu craned her neck as she lifted her gaze to meet Grim's. "Who called in the bouncer? Look, all I want is his autograph. Mitch Taylor said that he would sign my book, and that's what I want. With this."

She pulled a pen from her pocket and clicked a button on the side. With a *snick*, a four-inch blade extended from the tip.

People pulled away in surprise. Even Mitch cowered in his seat. His gaze bobbed around as if he was trying to figure out a way to leap out of his booth, over Lulu and out the door without losing a single drop of blood.

But she had him pinned. There was no place for him to escape.

Grim sighed as if he had so many better things to do and opened his palm. "Hand it over," he said in a bored voice.

Lulu clutched the penknife to her breast. "Over my dead body. He promised his signature."

Grim cocked a brow in disbelief. "And did he say that he'd do so in blood?"

"Yes."

"No," Mitch clarified. "I never said that I'd do it that way. She said that she wanted something special, after I'd already signed her copy of *Slasher of Sacrifice*." He added the title of his book in a proud, unapologetic way.

"That woman's crazy," Cammie said a little too loudly. The collective gaze of the room swiveled to my sister. She shrugged, lifted her glass and doubled down. "Yep. Crazy. Who has an author sign their name in blood?"

Lulu's cheeks puffed out like she'd stuffed them with marshmallows. Her eyes even bugged like a pug dog. I swear that her head trembled as if it were filling with steam and the woman was about to blow her top.

"What did you say?" Lulu demanded.

Cammie sucked her teeth. "I said that you were crazy."

With all the grace of a samurai warrior, Lulu arched the penknife in the air as she lunged for Cammie. Lucky for everyone in the room, Grim was quick as lightning. He reached out a hand, and magic snaked around her wrist.

"What's happening to me?" she said.

"You need to cool off." Grim told me, "I'll be right back."

He dragged Lulu from the restaurant, pulling her outside while she yelled that she needed Mitch's signature in blood.

I held my breath, waiting to see if anyone said one word about the magic that Grim had just used. According to him, regular folks couldn't see magic. When a witch or wizard used power, it appeared like a fog to people.

"Glad that's over," Cammie said. If anyone was going to say something about magic, it would have been my sister. I guessed she hadn't noticed Grim's power after all. "What a mess that woman is."

Pot calling kettle black, anyone? "I'm going to make sure Mitch is okay. Be right back."

The author was downing a shot glass full of brown liquid when I arrived at his table. He was seated with one of the men that I recognized from the library.

"This is Dr. Storm," Mitch said by way of introduction.

The professor took my hand. Even from where he sat, I could tell that he was tall as his long legs stretched out before him. His graying hair was clipped short and a small tuft of hair, a soul patch, sprouted from beneath his bottom lip.

"Nice to meet you," I said.

"The professor was integral to my research," Mitch said with an appreciative wave of his hand. "Without him, *Slasher of Sacrifice* never would've seen the light of day."

"Or the dead of night," Dr. Storm joked. "You know, seeing as the subject matter is so dark."

"What? Teenagers dying is dark?" I joked.

He chuckled lightly. "Pleasure to meet you, Mrs. Provey."

"Please, call me Paige."

Intrigue flared in his eyes. "Absolutely. *Paige.*"

A shiver raced down my spine as my name left his lips. Dr. Storm stared at me so long with those glittering eyes of his that in order to ease the tension, I blurted out, "So you were an integral part of Mitch's book?"

"Well, I wouldn't say integral," he said with the sort of bashfulness that I immediately understood as false.

"Nonsense." Mitch sipped a glass of water in front of him and wiped a sleeved arm over his mouth. "Without Dr. Storm, I never would've found the cave and the inscription that influenced the book's premise."

"Well," I said with a smile, "it's good to have friends who can help with your art."

Dr. Storm's eerie gaze made me feel like a thousand snakes slithered over my skin. It was time to go. "I just wanted to make sure that you were all right after what happened with Lulu. It was nice talking to you."

"Oh, don't go yet, Paige," Dr. Storm beckoned. "Tell me, have you had any influences over your art like my dear Mitch here? Any cave writings and inscriptions that have, shall we say, fed your muse?"

I laughed blithely. "No, no. No such interesting situations as that have helped with my work. I mostly just sit down and stories pop into my head. Well, most of the time."

He arched a graying brow. "Oh? Has something changed that for you of late?"

"I've had some writer's block." Why was I telling him this? Why did I feel the need to share the dirty details of my life with a man I'd only just met fifteen seconds earlier? "It usually passes quickly."

"But this one hasn't." Dr. Storm said it as a statement. "And you're worried."

Another chill swept down my arms. "I'm a bit worried. No writer likes to be cut off from the stories living inside of them. I'm no exception to that."

"You should come by my office. I can help with your block." At first I thought that Professor Storm was joking, so I laughed. But no one else at the table did. That was uncomfortable. When I realized that he wasn't joking, I did my best to play it off by touching a hand to my forehead. "Wow. Too much wine. It makes me think people are joking when they're actually serious."

Mitch patted Dr. Storm's shoulder. "Oh, the good professor isn't joking. He can help you. He helped me, didn't he? You'd be surprised by what all he can do. He'll change your life, that's for sure."

Dr. Storm shook his head. "Let's not get carried away, Mitch. Though I won't argue with you that I've certainly had some successes in my life."

"Well, thank you for the offer," I told him. But I wouldn't be taking advantage of it. There was no way that a creepy college professor could lift my temporary writer's block—especially not one who'd helped write a book called *Slasher of Sacrifice*. "Y'all have a nice evening."

They said goodbye and I made my way back to Cammie, only to find her leaning over the bar and touching noses with Ferguson.

I dropped my clutch purse loudly on the bar top. "What a night, wouldn't you say?"

Ferguson pulled back from my sister and wiped down the counter. "A little blood spilling is what makes a bar great, you know?"

I laughed. "That's funny. When I think of this place, I consider it more of a steak house than a bar."

"I don't." Cammie plucked an olive from a bowl in front of her and popped it into her mouth. "This is a bar."

I scoffed. "You just arrived ten seconds ago."

Ferguson shot Cammie a smile. "I'll be right back."

When he was gone, Cammie fixed her attention on me. "What's your problem?"

"Besides the fact that you're only here for a few days and you're already shacking up with Ferguson?"

"What's it to you?"

What *was* it to me? What did it matter what she did and who she did it with? Both Ferguson and she were adults. I was just the frustrated sister who couldn't get her own life together.

I sighed. "It's nothing. Do whatever you want to with him. But when you arrived, you said that you were here to see me. After what you told me tonight, I thought we might be on the road to healing."

She rolled an olive between her fingers. Just watching her made me hungry, so I grabbed one and tossed it into my mouth. Salty brine exploded on my tongue as my teeth crushed the tender flesh of the fruit.

"Man, that is good," I said with a moan.

"I know, right?" Cammie pushed the bowl toward me. "Have more."

"No, that's okay." A long silence ignited between us, and as distance sometimes softens people, time worked that same magic on my heart. Finally I said with a sigh, "Look, do whatever you want with Ferguson. He's barely a friend. But this town has a lot of surprises in it. Some of which I don't think you'll like."

"He's nice," she said quietly. The front door opened and she stiffened.

When I glanced over my shoulder, it was only Grim entering the bar. He came over and slid onto his stool with a huff. "That's over."

"Is Lulu gone?" I asked.

"About to be." He swiveled his body toward me. "Do we have time for one more drink before leaving?"

I rubbed his arm because I really just wanted to touch him. "Sure thing."

Thirty minutes later the bar was thinning out and a yawn snaked its way from my mouth.

"Tired?" Grim asked.

I nodded. "It's been a long day."

"Then let's get out of here."

He kept his hand on the small of my back as he guided me to the front door. I'd asked Cammie if she wanted to head out, but she was still too busy making googly eyes at Ferguson to leave.

Gosh, I hoped that man didn't get his heart broken. But as it was none of my business, I simply told them good night.

The humidity was so thick when we exited the restaurant that sweat immediately sprouted on my arms and upper lip. You had to love summers in the South. The air was so soupy you could swim through it.

Cicada trills and frog croaks overwhelmed the darkness, making the world seem like it was blanketed in the creatures.

"Beautiful night," Grim said.

"It is." My gaze swept the lot. It always amazed me how loud summer creatures could be, yet none of them were ever seen. "Wait. What's that?"

There was an odd shadow by one of the vehicles. It made the car look like it had a longer bumper than normal.

Grim noticed and frowned. "What *is* that?"

"You tell me."

As we neared, I couldn't shake the dread washing over my body, for as we closed in on the shadow, I saw a pair of feet sticking out from the car.

Grim threw out an arm and tried to keep me back, but I pushed my way to his side. Lightning crackled in his palm as he illuminated the body.

Lying on the ground as if in a deep sleep lay Lulu. But I knew better. Lulu wasn't steeped in slumber.

She was steeped in something else.

Death.

CHAPTER 10

Officer Cowan and the paramedics arrived within minutes. Much to my surprise, the paramedics declared that Lulu wasn't dead.

She was unconscious, but they weren't able to revive her at the scene. So they took her to the local hospital.

Officer Cowan interviewed us. He scratched his head as he listened to the story that Grim relayed.

"So you're telling me that this Lulu wanted the author's name in blood, had a penknife ready, and you talked her off that ledge."

Grim nodded. "She was fine when I left her."

"And where was that?"

"Out here. Outside. She was getting into her car."

"But you didn't see her drive off."

Grim's expression hardened. "I saw her put the vehicle in drive and rumble out of the parking lot."

Cowan jotted down on his notepad, *Victim left the scene.* He glanced up at Grim with a question in his eyes. "Did you see her return?"

"I didn't know that she had until we found her."

Cowan noted that, too. "And what would you say the victim's demeanor was this evening?"

"Annoyed," Grim told him in a tone that suggested he, too, was annoyed by Cowan. "This could be the work of a magical creature. People need to be alerted."

Cowan wrote that down as well. "Why would it have attacked her?"

"Because it's an evil creature without a brain," I suggested.

Cowan laughed and shook his head. "Ms. Provey, you have some very creative ideas seeing as how you're a writer and all. But when it comes to creatures, you've got a lot of learning to do."

I flashed Grim a confused look. "What does that mean?"

"It means that the officer and I have differing opinions."

"And what's that opinion?" I asked.

Grim gestured to Cowan. "He seems to think the aghash was not only a one-time thing, not worth worrying about, but also that it won't hurt regular people."

That was news to me. "Why won't it hurt people?"

"Because magical creatures are attracted to magical beings," Grim told me.

Oh, okay. That was news to me, but I was a juvenile when it came to all this magic business. Heck, I had witchy powers, but they only worked best when I was around another witch or wizard, and then they only copied what that person could do. It wasn't like I was any sort of master at my craft.

I wrapped my head around what Grim said and asked him, "Is that true?"

He slowly nodded. "Yes and no. They are attracted to people with magic." Cowan snorted and Grim shot him a look of death. "But that doesn't mean that something like an aghash wouldn't attack a human, especially if it was hungry enough."

"Chances of that are highly unlikely." Cowan rubbed his cheek with his pencil eraser. "Until we have reason to think we're dealing with anything other than a one-off, it's best we keep that information to ourselves. I'd hate to start a panic in the people."

"God forbid," Grim said dryly.

"But back to Miss Lulu. The last you saw of her—until she wound up on the ground—was her leaving the parking lot."

"That's right," Grim said.

Cowan scrunched up his face in question. "You got any reason to think why she'd return?"

Grim took my hand and started to pull me away. "No. For that answer, you'd have to ask her."

"I guess it's a good thing that she isn't dead then," Cowan said.

Grim nodded hard. "If there's anything else you need, call me."

As soon as we were out of earshot, I murmured, "You seem pretty annoyed with Cowan."

"Not annoyed. Just wish he'd see things my way." He swung a leg over the seat of his motorcycle and leveled the front wheel. I got on and laced my hands over his tight, tight abdomen. "But for this town's sake I hope that my instincts are wrong."

"How so?"

"Because if they're right, things may get bad." He started the engine and revved the motor. With a look over his shoulder, back at Cowan, Grim added, "Very, very bad."

THE NEXT MORNING, the very first email that I checked was from Madeleine. *Darling, how're the pages coming? What you've sent so far is brilliant. I can't wait to see more.*

I groaned and closed the email app. I was not ready to face her. I slowly pushed myself out of bed and realized that the smell of bacon frying and cooked eggs were coming from the tiny kitchen.

Great. I was so hungry. I pulled on a robe and headed out. "Cammie, I'm so glad you're making—"

I stopped talking because Cammie wasn't standing at my stove. Estelle Butts, my next-door neighbor (and I'm using the term *next-door* loosely as she lived half a mile away) was hovering over the burners.

"Morning," she said brightly.

"Morning," I replied hesitantly. I glanced around the cottage. "I'm not trying to be rude, but what're you doing here?"

Cammie exited the bathroom holding a bottle of my most expensive perfume. "I found it! Go ahead and try it on. This scent makes everyone smell good, and no man can resist you."

Snow appeared in the corner of the room, headfirst through the wall. "I considered waking you, but you looked like you were having a good slumber."

Cammie spotted me and grinned from ear to ear. "Well, it's about time you're up. Estelle's making us breakfast."

"I see that. Why?"

Estelle flashed me a grin as Cammie sprayed perfume on her neck. Very expensive perfume, I might add. It was $200 an ounce, and the only reason I had it was because I'd bought it a year ago and only used it sparingly. Since I couldn't afford it at the moment, I only wore it on very special occasions.

"We met yesterday," Cammie explained, "and just hit it right on off. I told her about your perfume that could attract any man, and Estelle wanted to smell it for herself. Said there's a fella in town she wants to hook."

"Yep, only man at the senior center not on a catheter." Estelle poured the skillet of eggs onto a plate. "He's a real catch."

"Sounds like," I muttered.

"You need more." Cammie lifted the bottle to spritz Estelle again, but before she could, I grabbed it. "Hey!"

"Sorry, but this is off-limits." I shoved the bottle into my pocket. "For now, at least."

"But what am I supposed to wear for my date with Ferguson tonight?" Cammie grumped.

"Don't know. Don't care."

"But that's what I wore last night to hook him."

I clenched and unclenched my fists in anger. "You wore my perfume? There's barely any left. Cammie, I'm saving it for special occasions."

"Meeting your soul mate is a special occasion," Estelle informed me.

At that, I laughed. "Ferguson is not Cammie's soul mate." The table had been set, and Estelle placed the plate of bacon in the middle. I sat and bit into a piece of the smoked meat. "In case my sister didn't tell you, she's only here for a few days. Not enough time to fall in love. Plus, I'm pretty sure she's a good head taller than him."

Cammie frowned. "Ferguson's as tall as I am." I shot her a dark look, and she quickly amended her statement to, "Okay, maybe he's a little shorter, but our lips touch okay."

My jaw dropped. "You kissed him?!"

She smiled slyly. "A girl never kisses and tells."

Estelle smirked. "Like I said, true love."

"Oh, goodness no. Cammie, you can't have a fling with Ferguson."

She blinked at me blankly. "Why not?"

"Because…" My sister sat across the table, her dyed-black hair piled high on her head, big hoop earrings dangling from her ears and her lipstick already applied. Even though we were from two different planets, I couldn't blurt out the truth about Ferguson.

Estelle poured coffee into the cup by my plate. "Yes, Paige. Why don't you tell us why Cammie can't fall in love with Ferguson."

I threw her a scathing look. That old woman knew why. She was magical, could control vegetation. And she knew that I was magical, too. And I suspected, from the twinkle in her eye, that Estelle knew that I knew that she knew that Cammie *wasn't* magical.

Whew. My brain exploded just a little thinking that last sentence.

"Because," I said slowly, trying to pick the perfect words, "like I said, Cammie won't be in town long enough to find out that Ferguson is her soul mate. Besides, I think my sister's already had one or two of those."

Estelle wagged her brows. "Mr. No Catheter will be my fourth soul mate if I'm lucky. Or if he is."

Lawd, it was way too early in the morning to have that conversation.

From the corner Snow said, "I'm going to head out, get from fresh air."

"Lucky," I murmured.

"What's that?" Cammie asked.

"Nothing." Deciding the best course of action was a diversion, I said, "Thank you for making this great breakfast, Estelle. I appreciate it."

"Well, you're welcome. It's from one witch to another."

My stomach tightened. "I don't know about all that," I grumbled as Cammie's eyes popped wide with interest.

"Well, you can be a bit of the B word," my sister said with a laugh. "I guess that lines up with being a witch."

I shot Estelle a look that told her to be quiet, and she shrugged, not caring. But Cammie wasn't finished.

"Estelle, are you a witch?"

"Well, um…"

"I think it's so neat what these modern-day witches do with crystals and everything. They get it right. Not like those old types of witches that Hollywood promotes—you know, the kind that don't really exist. I mean, no one can shoot thunderbolts from their fingers or make trees grow. They make witches look like superheroes. Nothing like that exists, and if it did, it shouldn't. No one needs that kind of power."

"No?" Estelle asked.

Cammie chewed a big bite of eggs. I never understood how my sister could eat whatever she wanted and not gain an ounce. Talk about superpowers.

"Course not," Cammie continued. "What if the bad guys had the ability to shoot lasers from their fingers? What would stop a good guy from becoming bad? People would fill your head with nonsense like you're some kind of demigod. No, thank you. I'm so happy that witches and wizards with big huge powers don't exist. Because if I ever met one, I'd be forced to do one thing."

"What's that?" I asked.

"Well," Cammie said, leaning back and hooking her thumbs onto her belt loops, "I would take them out."

I laughed. "Honestly? Take a witch out?"

"Yep. Anyone comes toward me with lasers shooting from their fingers and they're getting this." She crossed to her duffel bag, unzipped it and dipped her hand in. When Cammie pulled it out, she was holding a snub-nosed revolver. "I'd pop that sucker with a few of these. Nope. Nobody needs that kind of power. Nobody."

The hair on the back of my neck rose. Since when had my sister become a homicidal maniac?

CHAPTER 11

*A*fter breakfast, Estelle quickly washed everything up and left, leaving me with my sister, who I wasn't sure how to take after that whole conversation with the gun.

She sat at the table with her phone in her hands, scrolling through a social media app.

"So," I said tentatively, unsure how I was going to feel my way through this conversation, "you have a gun."

Her back stiffened. "Yep."

I slipped onto the seat beside her. "Is there a reason for that?"

"Self-protection." Her gaze flickered to me. "You cain't never be too careful going into these Podunk towns. You know what I mean?"

"Yeah." I laughed feebly. "I sure do. But um, even if these Podunk towns have criminals and you need protection, I'm surprised you didn't mention the gun before."

She shrugged. "Why would I have?"

"Well, I don't know…because it's a gun in my house."

"This ain't your house."

"I'm renting it for the summer."

My sister glared at me. "Like I said, it ain't yours."

"You're right, it isn't. But I still live here, and it would have been nice to know about the weapon."

"Well, now you know, and knowing is half the battle. Sheesh. You have lost your Southern. You should be packing heat, too. Besides, after what happened last night, I would think that you'd be thanking me."

"You're kidding, right?"

"That Lulu woman was obviously attacked. If she'd been with me, I would've pulled my gun out to help her."

Alarm bells rang in my head. "You had that weapon with you last night?"

"Of course. Take it with me wherever I go. A girl's gotta look after herself. Be prepared in case anything bad happens."

"Yeah, I guess so," I muttered. "But I still don't like it. I'd prefer if you got rid of it."

Okay, I know there was no real reason for me to worry. Humans couldn't actually see magic. That was proven. Cammie hadn't seen the lasers that shot from Grim's hand back at the restaurant the night before, because if she had, my sister would've blown a hole through him, as she had so kindly told me.

What worried me was that I had magic. And perhaps Cammie, if around me long enough, might begin to see things, hear things. Would she blow me into next week if she discovered the truth?

"Cammie, what if someone close to you had magic?"

"Huh?"

I tapped the top of her phone to get her attention. "You said that you'd shoot anyone with magic. Well, what if someone close to you had it? Someone really close?"

Her eyes narrowed to slitty wedges. "What if they did?"

"Would you hurt them?"

"Depends." She considered it. "Nah. I'd get rid of them. Like I said, all that power cain't be good for nobody. They start to think they're above the law."

"Wouldn't you be above the law if you shot someone who had magic?"

Cammie scoffed. "First of all, I don't know why we're even having this conversation because magic ain't real. Secondly, my closeness to someone wouldn't change nothing. Anyone with that kind of power would be bad for humanity. I'd be doing the world a favor."

"You'd be committing murder."

She slipped her phone into her pocket and rose. "It ain't like any of this is gonna happen, Paige. I don't know why you're so worried about it." A knock came from the door. "I'll get it," she informed me.

Go ahead, make yourself at home. Answer my door. Invite people I barely know over. Oh, and while you're at it, threaten to destroy most of the entire town of inhabitants.

"Why, hey, Abe. How're you?"

Cammie stepped from the door and in trotted Abraham, Patricia's nephew. He carried a paper sack that sagged at the bottom.

"Morning, Miss Cammie, Miss Paige. I got all the things you asked for, Miss Cammie. But the grocery store didn't have the caviar you asked for. Mr. Humphries, the owner, told me you'd have to go to the next town to find that."

Cammie tittered. "Oh, that's okay. I guess that I can do without my caviar."

"Caviar?" I laughed. "Since when have you started eating caviar?"

My sister shot me a perturbed look. "Since for a long time now. You don't know everything about me, Paige. Remember? We're supposed to be using this time to bond."

"Over caviar?"

"Well, obviously not now."

Abe pulled a slim rectangular box from the sack. "But I did find those expensive crackers you wanted, and that cheese. Boy, whoever would've thought that cheese could cost thirty dollars a pound. Got you half a pound of it. I hope that's enough."

"Oh, yes, that's plenty." Cammie shooed Abe from the sack and smiled. "Don't worry about the rest of it. I'll get it."

"Great." Abe handed her the receipt, which she crumpled and punched into her pocket. "Just let me know if you need anything else. The grocery store has your credit card on file now. They have no problem charging it whenever you need anything."

"Oh, thank you so much."

Abe stood there awkwardly. Cammie watched him, and then she nodded to me. "Miss Paige has your tip."

Oh, I did, did I? Instead of arguing, I dug into my purse and found a couple of bucks.

"Here you go. Thank you."

Abe folded the bills and tucked them neatly into his shirt pocket. "Thank *you* very much, Miss Paige. Oh, and Miss Cammie, I can bike over to the next town and pick up that caviar for you."

She giggled nervously. "That won't be necessary. I'll let you know if there's anything else I need."

"And I couldn't get the champagne because I'm not old enough yet," Abe told her. "The grocery store lady wouldn't let me buy it."

Cammie shook her head and scowled. "Did you tell them it was for me?"

"Sure did, but they didn't care. Said something about the law being the law."

She scooted him toward the door. "Ain't that a shame? Well, thanks again." With that, Abe stepped out into the morning, and Cammie shut the door behind him. "I thought that kid would never leave."

I quirked a brow. "Getting groceries delivered? And expensive stuff, too. Since when is caviar a Southern thing? Maybe *you've* lost *your* Southern."

"Like that could happen." She scoffed. "You're the one who needs help in that department."

I peered into the sack. There was cheese, crackers, grapes, sparkling cider and cuts of expensive deli meat. "This is quite the spread. I didn't know you had a charcuterie board in you."

Cammie snatched the sack away. "For your information, I have many talents."

"Good to know."

"And none of this can be touched because it's for my date with Ferguson tonight."

My eyes nearly popped from my head. "Date?"

"Yep." Cammie lifted her nose with pride. "I've got a date with Fergie. Told him that I'd fix something nice for us."

I didn't know why I was surprised. She should have fun with the bartender because in a few days she'd be gone and I wouldn't have a bullet in my arm—none of us would. The town would be safe from my demented sister.

"That's great," I told her. "I'm sure you'll have a good time with him. Ferguson's a nice person."

"We hit it off. He is like the cream to my Oreos, the jam between my peanut-buttered slices of bread. We click, you know?"

"Yeah, I know." I pointed to the sack of goodies. "Y'all have a good time. I'm sure Ferguson would love to have you over to cook."

I headed back to my bedroom to get dressed (yes, I was still in my robe), when Cammie's voice stopped me.

"Oh, well, um, Paige?"

"Hmm?"

"There seems to be a bit of a miscommunication here."

I turned around. "There does?"

"Yeah." She twisted her fingers. "You see, I'm not going to Ferguson's."

"You're not?"

"No." Cammie grimaced. "I invited him here for dinner. At six. He'll probably stay several hours. Is that okay?"

"Sure." I dismissed her concern with a wave. "I can pop out for a while. Be back around eight." Her expression fell and I rolled my eyes. "Okay. So you need me back later? How about nine? Ten?"

"I was thinking more like midnight."

"Midnight? Cammie, what are you and Ferguson going to do from six until midnight?" Before she answered, I lifted my hand in a stop motion. "Never mind. As long as nothing happens on my bed, I'm okay with it. Look, I can't promise that I'll be gone until midnight. But I can leave for a couple of hours."

"Three?" she squeaked.

"Two," I insisted as I walked into my room. "And not a minute longer."

With that, I shut my door.

CHAPTER 12

I'd just gotten dressed when my phone rang. My heart lurched at the name splashed across the screen—*Grim*.

Not wanting to seem desperate (even though I clearly was when it came to him), I let the phone ring three times before answering. Could have let it go more, but then I risked Grim going to voice mail, and I didn't want to wait three or four hours to call him back.

"Hello?"

"Hey, how're you today?" he said in his smexy voice.

"I'm good. And you?"

"Just heard from Cowan."

"Oh? Is he going to let people know about the aghash?"

"Not at all. Ferguson is putting something together about that."

"Good."

He exhaled and I could almost feel his breath coming across the line and tickling my face. "I'm calling about Lulu."

My stomach tightened. "Is she…is she going to make it?"

"She's in a coma."

That confused me. "A coma? Did she hit her head when she fell? I assumed she was attacked. Did her assailant push her to the ground?"

"You assumed the same things I did—attack and burglary. But she had her purse."

"Was it a heart attack?"

I'd never heard of a heart attack putting a person in a coma, but I supposed there was a first time for everything.

"No," he confirmed. "Not that, either."

Now I was super confused. "Then what happened?"

"Doctors don't know. They've run every scan they can, checked her blood chemistry and it's all within normal limits."

"It's not related to diabetes, is it?" When doing research for a book once, I remembered reading about how if a diabetic's blood sugar got too high, or even too low, they could wind up in a coma. But then the lab results would've detected that easily, so I said, "I guess not if the docs didn't find anything on her blood panel."

"It's a coma that no one can explain. But I learned that she was at the library for the book signing."

"That's right."

"Did you see anything strange while she was there?"

I folded my arms and said slyly, "Mr. Grim, are you doing the investigating in this case or is Cowan?"

"I'm helping."

Then the real reason why he was so interested hit me. "You're afraid it could've been a creature from the book, aren't you?"

"Among other things," he admitted, sounding particularly sour that he'd had to.

My stomach knotted even more than it already was. "Let me think about the reading…yes, Lulu was there. She had an argument with…"

"With you?" he asked.

"Not with me."

Saying *with my sister* was a bad idea. Cammie had left the restaurant before we had last night, and she hadn't gone with Ferguson. Don't ask me how she managed to peel herself off him. I guessed it was because she had tonight and her charcuterie board of love to look forward to.

Then I thought about Cammie and her smoking gun of hate and my writer's imagination went insane in the membrane. What if Lulu had magic and Cammie discovered that and shot her. But wait—Lulu hadn't been wounded by a firearm. Unless…

Before Grim could ask any more about the argument, I steered the conversation in a different direction. "Did Lulu have any impact wounds?" I asked, crossing my fingers that my theory was way off base.

"Lump on the back of her head. The doctors don't know if she got it before or after the fall."

"They're doctors, not forensic pathologists, and lucky for us, Lulu isn't dead."

"It *is* lucky if a creature attacked her," he grumbled.

A creature or my sister. What if Cammie had met Lulu outside and they'd gotten into another argument? What if it wasn't even about magic? What if Lulu just made Cammie angry and she pistol-whipped her?

My breath came out shaky. How could I think such things about Cammie? Never had I known Cammie to act violently. But I also had only discovered that she owned a gun. If she was willing to shoot a witch simply for having magic, was it such a far cry to think that maybe, just maybe my sister would hit a woman over the head with said weapon, especially after an argument?

No, it wasn't. In fact, it was so close-fetched that if it had been a snake, it would've bit me.

"The main reason I called," Grim told me, "is to say, be careful, and if anything strange happens, let me know. Nothing is too small."

Now how sweet was that? He was just calling to say that he wanted me to be safe. My heart swelled just a bit. "I'll be careful."

"And it wouldn't hurt for you to learn more about how to work your magic."

Right. "I mean, if you've got it, you should flaunt it, right?"

"No, not like that," he said darkly.

"That doesn't apply here? Flaunting magic isn't a good thing?"

"Flaunting anything is never good."

Note to self—do not flaunt in front of Grim. "All right. Will not flaunt magic. But can you at least get me to the point where I can show it off a bit?"

"Babe," he said, which made my stomach swallow my heart, "you can show off whatever you want around me."

"But I thought that I wasn't supposed to flaunt anything. Now I'm confused."

"Flaunting is different."

"No, it isn't."

"Sure it is."

"Okay, but I don't know how."

"I'll show you sometime," he threatened in a way that made me want to leap through the phone and let him demonstrate the difference right then and there. "As for your magic, let's get together soon. How about tomorrow?"

"I can do tomorrow." Tonight would've been better as I was getting kicked out of my rental, but I kept that to myself. "You name the place and I'll be there."

"My place. I'll pick you up."

"What time?"

"Six thirty? I'll even have dinner ready."

Happiness that manifested in warmth spread over my chest. "Dinner? What did I ever do to deserve such good treatment?"

"I like you. I don't like everyone, but you're an exception."

My mouth was smiling so wide that my entire face ached. "I will take whatever exception that I can."

"Good. Also, wear loose-fitting clothing."

Really? I was dying to make a joke about that one—being on a date with him, wearing loose-fitting clothing…did that entail crotchless panties, too?

But good girls didn't say things like that. So instead I just replied, "Got it—sweatpants, that sort of thing," I joked. I mean, no one wore sweatpants on a date.

"Sweats are perfect. You'll be working hard."

Wait. Was this a date or a training session? Dinner was involved, which screamed *date,* and clearly crotchless panties had been banned. But sweatpants were a must, and nobody looked sexy in sweats. I didn't care what they wore on top of them, they were not sexy.

I decided to wear leggings instead. That way, I could still pump up the beauty factor while maintaining the comfort needed for training.

Also, I might put on the crotchless panties.

You know, just in case.

We said goodbye and I quickly set aside the clothing that I was going to wear the next evening so that I'd easily be able to find them. With that completed, I got dressed and readied to face the day.

The day itself went quickly. I spent most of it at home, staring at my computer screen. When I found myself getting peckish, I attempted to sneak a small hunk of the cheese Cammie'd had delivered, but she'd caught me and forced me to put it back.

After I'd already pulled it off.

"Fix that like you found it," she demanded.

I pinched the small hunk of cheddar between my thumb and forefinger. "But…it's off the block."

She folded her arms. "I don't care. Put it back like you found it right now. Or else."

"Or else what?"

"You don't want to find out."

And then I remembered the gun and Lulu and I did exactly as my sister had said. "What's up with you? Why're you so testy? Are you feeling okay? Is there something that you want to talk about?"

"There ain't nothing I want to talk about. I just want you to stay away from my cheese."

I lifted my hands in surrender. "All right, will do."

"And are you planning to be gone tonight?"

I sighed, completely annoyed. "Yes, I plan to be gone."

But I had to make sure that Cammie was watched. She wouldn't harm Ferguson because she liked him (way too much). But I still wanted eyes on her. I just needed to find a way to go about it.

Just then, Snow popped her head through the wall. "Is it quieter in here yet?" When I didn't answer she floated inside. "Thank goodness, it is. Way too much excitement earlier. I like things calm and cool."

"And don't come back too early," Cammie told me.

An idea formed inside my head. "I don't plan to."

When Cammie's back was turned, I wiggled my finger at Snow and motioned for her to follow me into my bedroom.

"Everything okay?" she asked once we were closed up inside.

I lowered my voice to a whisper. "I need a favor."

"Sure." She sat on the edge of my bed. I didn't know why she did that. She didn't need to sit or sleep. "What is it?"

"Stay here tonight and keep an eye on Cammie."

"Okay."

I couldn't simply let Snow do the favor without knowing every dirty detail. I blew out a breath and confessed, "She's having a man over."

Snow shrugged like it was no big deal. "No problem."

I hated that I even had to say the next part. "They might do things."

"Like play board games?"

"No, like *other* things." I shot her a look that hopefully conveyed what I meant. "Very adult sort of things."

"Oh. Oh!" Snow grimaced. "I'm sorry, but I forgot that I have to wash my hair tonight."

"You're a ghost!"

"It's an air wash. It still gets that not so fresh smell if I don't let it air out. Takes hours."

I reached for her, and my hand passed straight through her arm. "Snow, please. I need you to do this for me. I can't stay here. She'll know if I'm peeping through the windows."

"Who're you talking to in there?" Cammie called.

"Just my agent. I'm on the phone with her!" Back to Snow, I was not above begging. "Please. I'm worried about my sister, that she may be involved in something."

Snow gave me a sulking look before exhaling heavily. "Fine. I'll do it. But you owe me."

"Whatever you want. Thank you." I opened my arms to sweep her into a hug and stopped. "Since I can't embrace you, how about an air hug?"

She opened her arms and we mock hugged. With Snow watching Cammie, everything would be fine. Tonight would be perfect.

Just wait and see.

CHAPTER 13

*C*ammie couldn't shoo me out the door fast enough. "Don't be back before nine. I mean it. No telling what you'll walk in on. I might be hand-feeding Ferguson."

That was the least of my worries. I'd be elated to intrude on that. "I'll stay out," I promised.

Snow spied me from the kitchen. "If I see one thing that I don't want to, you're going to hear all the dirty details!"

Though I figured Snow meant that to sound like a warning, it came out more like a promise. Hmm. Perhaps Snow was a bit too eager for this job after all.

But there was no time to worry about that as Cammie slammed the door in my face, leaving me outdoors. I got into my vehicle and steered it toward town, trying to figure out how to entertain myself for the next few hours.

I HEADED to the nearest coffee shop, Banshee Beans, ordered a muffin and a coffee and aimed myself toward a table in the back.

I'd brought my computer with me so that I could stare at the screen for the next couple of hours, wishing that an idea of where to go next in my book would pop into my head.

My heroine was living under a curse that forced her to be apart from the man she loved every day of the year except for one. That night had arrived, and this year, she was going to do everything in her power to break the curse.

And that was as far as I'd gotten. Nothing else was coming to me— no ideas on how to break the curse, or even who the supporting characters were—and I still had three quarters of a book to write.

Madeleine had adored what I'd written so far. But I couldn't admit I'd pushed my brain as far as it would go—my creative well was dry. No, I needed to pull two hundred more pages from my imagination well and slap those puppies onto the page if it killed me.

My gaze snagged on a bulletin board as I walked toward a table in the coffee shop. There were flyers plastered all over it, but what caught my attention was a paper shimmering with magic. Green sparkles shot from the edges like tiny fireworks.

AGHASH DISCOVERED IN WILLOW LAKE! RESIDENTS BE CAREFUL.

The copy beneath the headline detailed what had occurred when Grim was attacked by the monster. People were being told not to stay out late and to travel in groups if possible. No one knew if the aghash was a one-time occurrence or if another monster would appear, so residents were warned to be safe rather than sorry.

Before I could skim the rest of it, a voice came from behind me. "And how is the writing going, Ms. Provey?"

I turned to see Professor Storm hovering nearby, paper cup of coffee in hand.

I sighed, deflated. "Not so great. Wish that I could say otherwise."

His mouth quirked in an expression that hinted on amusement. Was my pain and suffering funny to him?

"Like I said the other night, I'd be happy to help you."

"Well, if you can plot out the rest of my story, I'll take that," I joked.

"This is no laughing matter," he chastised.

"Oh." I straightened, not used to being reprimanded. "It's not?"

"No." He placed the coffee on a nearby table and approached. Before I could move, Dr. Storm had his fingertips on my head and was massaging my scalp. "I can help unlock your potential. I did the same for Mitch Taylor, and you see how well his book is doing."

I scoffed. "Yeah, right. Who in the world is really going to buy a book titled *Slasher of Sacrifice?*"

"It's already hit the USA Today bestseller list."

I jerked from his hands. "It has?"

"No, but it could." He wiggled his fingers. "Let me help you."

I had to admit, the massage had immediately relaxed me. Perhaps it was what I needed. A little bit of relaxation and the words would flow smoothly.

"Okay," I relented.

He smiled. "Let's meet in my office."

"Can we do it now?" When he hesitated, I begged, "I've got to get this book to my agent. Please."

Dr. Storm smiled. "Certainly. Why not?"

THE PROFESSOR'S office was filled with crystal skulls and ancient arrowheads and cracked pieces of pottery.

"These are from this area," he explained.

"Even the skulls?"

"Not those." He picked one up and cradled it to his chest. "This I bought while overseas. Did you know that crystals house all the knowledge of the world?"

Okay, crazy man. "I didn't realize that."

He stroked the silky pate of the skull. "They are powerful objects, able to heal and help, give clarity and restore inner peace."

"Wow, all that and also in the shape of a head," I remarked. "Whoever would have thought it?"

"The ancients did," he mused. The professor kept sweeping his hand down the skull and looking at me as if this was an actual conversation. "The ancients understood the potential of the crystals, their use in healing and magic." He said the last word mystically. "You understand magic."

He waited for me to answer, but I wasn't comfortable admitting that I'd recently discovered my power. I couldn't tell who was a witch and who wasn't, not without them admitting it to me. And humans couldn't actually see witches using magic, so discussing my abilities with any old Joe Shmoe was a big no-no.

So in reply to his statement about me understanding magic, I laughed and slapped the air with my hand. "I don't know about all that. I've written about ghosts in the past. Got me into a lot of trouble."

"Please sit," he commanded, gesturing to an antique chair with thick wooden arms and legs. The seat cushion was threaded in horsehair so shiny and slick that I was sure my butt would slide right off. When I hesitated, the professor repeated his request again.

So I sat.

He continued to pet the crystal. "You've only gotten into trouble because there was some disconnection between your life and what your readers *believed* was your life."

That was true. My readers had believed that I could see ghosts, talk to them, that sort of thing, and I hadn't been the best at clarifying the truth. And now that I was able to communicate with the other side, I couldn't just say, *Hey, guys, look! I can see ghosts now. You don't have to cancel me! You can still love me the way that you did before!*

"I imagine," the professor continued, "that caused a lot of stress in your life, your readers turning their backs on you."

"It did," I admitted quietly. "But what's done is done."

He kept on, still stroking that head he held. "And I imagine that stress made it hard to think, to write, to come up with anything new."

"I managed that, but now I'm stuck in the middle of a story."

After you'd written several books, it became hard to come up with new ideas, new twists. That was my problem now. Did I reuse an old plot vehicle that I'd done before?

"Just breathe," he commanded. "And close your eyes."

"You're not going to stick that skull on my head, are you?" I half-joked.

"No, I'm not."

I closed my eyes, relieved. "Okay, good."

"I'm going to press it to your lips."

My lids popped open. "What?" There was no telling how many lips it had touched. There were a lot of germs in the world. I didn't want to catch anything that could kill me. The skull edged closer, and I pushed it away. "I don't know about all that, now."

"It won't hurt," he promised. "And I only just wiped it clean this morning with some water and sand—sand purifies. Lots of healing microbes in it."

The professor stared down at me so earnestly, and I'd come all this way. I might as well go along with it. What did I have to lose? Especially since he'd cleaned the thing with sand.

That was sarcasm.

"Okay. Have at it," I said reluctantly.

"Close your eyes."

I did so and a second later the cold crystal touched my lips. A shiver grabbed hold of my body, working its way down to my toes. It wasn't the temperature of the crystal that had caused my reaction. It was something deep inside the rock.

Don't ask me how I knew that, but I did.

Once the shiver was gone, I adjusted to the smooth surface against my mouth. Since the rock was supposed to hold all the knowledge and secrets of the universe, I expected to feel that in its touch—maybe some humming, possibly a buzzing against my skin.

But I didn't experience a dang thing.

I sat there with my eyes closed wondering how long the frigid crystal would be touching me, and how could I politely leave the professor, and what all did I have to do tomorrow and I prayed that no one's naked butt was on top of my bed at that moment.

Hopefully Snow would come up with a distraction to stop that from happening.

But I hadn't told her so. Crap. Why hadn't I instructed Snow to stop Cammie from desecrating my sheets at all costs? How could I have been so stupid?

"How do you feel?" the professor asked.

My lids popped open. "Great. I feel great."

Must've been the Southern in me. We folks in the South always tell others we're doing great, even when we're dying on the inside. Don't know why that is, but that's how things go.

Ha. See? I hadn't lost my Southern.

He placed the crystal back on a shelf. "You're all done. That should help open up the pathways for creativity. Sometimes when stress or trauma affects a person, the lines from the creative side of the brain become jammed up. The crystal skull will open those, allowing for the ease of information to pass through. It should also spark new thoughts, fresh ideas."

All I felt was relief that the moment was over and that I didn't have a rock pressed to my lips anymore.

I rose. "Great. Thank you. I appreciate your help."

He took my hand. "You may have a lot of energy in the upcoming hours. Don't forget to rest."

It took all I had not to quirk a brow in disbelief. Energy? From that encounter? Bah. Humbug.

I thanked Dr. Storm and left, heading back to my car. I glanced at my watch. It was barely seven thirty. I still had time to kill before Cammie would allow me home. Perhaps I'd return to the coffee shop and grab a sandwich for dinner.

While I was driving back, thinking of how silly it was that a crystal could do anything other than simply sit and be a rock, the book I was writing popped into my head.

I saw, like in a movie reel, my heroine, her hero and the curse that separated them. The story unfurled like a great red ribbon, taking me past the curse to their meeting and her figuring out how to stop it.

And I had it! I had the middle of my book, and I had the ending! If I didn't start getting words down right that minute, I'd lose it—all of it.

I slowed near the coffee shop and was going to stop, but I needed my own space, my own room to really get the story down.

As much as I knew my sister would hate it, I was on my way to crash her date.

CHAPTER 14

I hauled butt to the cabin. A dim light burned inside, a romantic one, one that could have been created by draping a scarf over a lamp. Perhaps there were also candles. Maybe Abe had delivered those earlier along with the outrageously expensive cheese; I simply hadn't seen it.

I killed the engine, grabbed my computer and charged toward the cabin. I gave a good hard knock on the door and then forged ahead inside.

Cammie screamed. Out of my peripheral vision I saw two bodies on the couch. They looked intertwined, but I didn't put my full gaze on them to make sure.

They may also have been clothed or unclothed. Once again, uncertain.

"What're you doing here?" my sister screeched.

"Got to work. Don't mind me!" I headed past them and into my bedroom, where I shut the door.

I found Snow on my bed. "I came in here a while ago. Sorry, but I couldn't take it out there any longer," she admitted.

As much as I wanted to know all the dirty details (or didn't want to know, let's be honest), there were other things on my mind. "Not now. Gotta write."

I opened my computer, slid a pair of noise-canceling headphones over my ears and tuned into the book that sat on my laptop.

I don't know how long I wrote for, but Dr. Storm's warning that I would have a ton of energy seemed to be true. I was filled to the brim with ideas. The words poured from me, and when I glanced up, finally, from the screen, the windows were brightening.

Dawn had arrived and I'd written all night. Finally exhausted, I shut my laptop, pulled the covers over my head, and slept.

When I awoke hours later, my phone was ringing. My eyes flared open in fright from being wakened from a dead sleep. My mind was fuzzy and thick. And that was how I answered the phone.

"Hello?"

"Darling, it's me, Madeleine. How're things?"

I bolted up. "Madeleine?"

"Yes, your agent," she snipped. "You know, the one person who believes in your career and that you can rebound from this whole canceling business. *That* Madeleine."

"Right." The fog quickly vanished from my brain as if it had been sucked up with a vacuum. "Yes, sorry. I just woke up. I wrote all night."

"Finally, some good news," she said with a sigh of relief. "I was beginning to think that you were avoiding me."

Absolutely. "Never. I wouldn't do that."

"I won't mention the fact that you've been dodging my calls. Not worth my time. But I'm hoping that since you were writing, that you've got something to show me. Your editor is breathing down my neck. This book is due soon, Paige. She wants to make sure that you're going to be on schedule. And to be honest, I feel like I've been lying for you, saying that it'll be ready. But even I'm not sure."

Oh no. I'd really been slacking. I sat up straighter, threw my shoulders back. "It's going to be on time. I promise."

"I want to see pages."

I hated where our relationship had fallen to. Used to be that Madeleine trusted my instincts. But ever since my falling out with my fan base and my publisher threatening to drop me, she had been looking over my shoulder.

"I've got pages for you. They're unedited."

"Darling, I don't care. Send me anything and everything you've got."

81

I'd left my laptop on the bed last night. I opened it and located what I'd written only the night before. "Sending it now. Tell me when the email hits your inbox."

I sent the file, and a few moments later Madeleine said, "Got it. I'll read over and let you know what I think. *Ciao,* darling. Talk soon."

She ended the call abruptly, and I exhaled and fell onto the headboard.

My clock read ten o'clock and since I was wide awake, though working on little sleep, I decided to start my day.

I pulled on my robe and headed into the living room to find Cammie seething at the table. "What…just what was that about last night?"

I halted and stared at her. What had I done, again? "Sorry I came home early." Thinking my apology was enough, I moved to brew a cup of coffee. "It was just that I met up with this professor who used a crystal to unlock the words in my head." I dumped grounds into the Keurig, hit the start button and turned to talk to my sister. "You wouldn't believe it, but he used some sort of crazy crystal skull on me, and it completely cured my writer's block. I was able to get a whole lot of work done."

Cammie stared at me with a sour expression glued to her face. "You ruined my date."

Before I could stop it, a laugh bubbled from me. "Are you sure about that? Because from the way things looked, y'all were hot and heavy. Not that I saw anything," I quickly added. "But it seemed like there was a lot of flesh going on."

"There would have been more if you hadn't come home," she grumbled.

So I'd actually made her angry. "Look, Cammie. I'm sorry. But this is my cabin."

"It's your rental," she said with a salty voice. "You don't own it."

"And neither do you." My coffee finished brewing, and I opened the fridge and grabbed the cream. While I doctored my drink, I said with as much restraint as possible, "You showed up on my doorstep with no explanation except that you wanted to hang out. Well, how much hanging out have we actually done? You've been busy hitting on men."

She rose from the chair, face red. "And you've been busy going on dates."

"You showed up without asking. Yes, I already had plans. What do you expect me to do, stop the world for you? This isn't about you, Cammie. I came here to write a book, to attempt to salvage my career."

"What about our sistership? What about salvaging that?"

"When have we ever had a relationship?" Her gaze cut to the floor. "There has been plenty of time to spend together, and suddenly now it's important that we bond and let bygones be bygones?"

"Better late than never," she explained.

"Cammie, what are you really doing here? You didn't come to vacation with me."

She rubbed her arms. "Like I said, I just needed to get away, and I wanted to see you."

I threw out my hands. "Well, you're seeing me. Get a good look, and don't be pissed off if I interrupt you having sex with the town bartender on my couch."

Her jaw unhinged. "We weren't having sex."

I glared at her.

Her voice dropped. "Okay, we might have been about to, but we hadn't yet."

Our gazes met and we both laughed. It was such a ridiculous situation—my middle-aged sister about to screw a leprechaun on the couch right before I barged in. She must've thought the entire thing was funny, too, because she sank back onto her chair.

"Please tell me that I can lay on that couch without pressing my skin to body fluids," I said.

She laughed. "Yes, you can. No fluids were exchanged."

"Thank goodness." I took my coffee cup to the table and sat across from her. "I am sorry about last night."

Cammie cocked an interested brow. "Who'd you say that you were with?"

"Oh, this professor named Dr. Storm. He was at the restaurant the other night with Mitch Taylor. He wore a jacket and was tall, balding."

"I remember him," she said dryly. "He and I may need to have a little chat."

She was joking, so I laughed. "Sorry. I really wasn't trying to intrude."

"Sure you weren't. You wanted to catch Fergie naked; I know you did."

I burst into a fit of laughter. "Trust me, I don't."

She sat back and studied me. "Say, are you hungry?"

My stomach growled on cue. I hadn't eaten supper and had stayed up all night working. I was famished. "Yes."

A conspiratorially spark glinted in her eyes. "What do you say we go get some ice cream?"

"I know a place."

"Do they have toppings?"

"They do." Along with blood ice cream, but I left that out.

"Great." She patted her stomach. "Because I could go for some chocolate and gummy worms."

We used to put gummy worms in our ice cream when we were kids. It had been so long since we'd done so, that I'd nearly forgotten about that. "You know what, that sounds great. Let's get dressed and head into town."

Half an hour later we were sitting inside of Palmer's. I had a bowl of butterscotchy butter pecan in front of me, and Cammie had chocolate topped with gummy worms.

She eyed my bowl. "You didn't get any worms."

"I wasn't sure how'd they go with this flavor."

"They'd go amazing." She plucked several from her bowl and dropped them into mine. "Try them."

I scraped a bit of ice cream onto my spoon and curled a gummy worm on top. When the combination of buttery cream and fruity gummy hit my tongue, it brought back memories of Saturday afternoons as kids sitting at our local Woolworth's department store (before they went out of business), eating a cheeseburger that was made on the grill in front of us and then finishing off our treat with ice cream and gummy worms.

There was nothing like being a kid on a Saturday back then. Those were the best memories.

"This is good," I told my sister.

"It's so good," she confirmed, moaning as she slid the spoon into her mouth. "We should do this every day."

I laughed. "My waistline wouldn't like it very much."

"But your tastebuds would." A silence fell between us for a stretch before Cammie said, "Why is it that we don't get along? Why're we so distant?"

It was one thing to think a certain thing, another for it to be said and placed out in the open. Cammie'd had the courage to express what I knew, and for that I wasn't sure if I was ashamed or if I was relieved that the friction between us was out in the open.

"I suppose part of it is because I just wanted to be your little sister, someone who you were friends with, and for our entire lives I felt like you saw me as so much less than you. I was never old enough to hang out or be one of your friends, someone you actually liked. I was just a second-class citizen, a kid not cool enough to be more."

Cammie's face crumpled. "That's what you thought?"

"Yes. Don't you remember how I followed you around? I was a little puppy dog, wanting to be accepted. And when I finally thought that I had been, the tables got turned on me and you told everyone that I wasn't anything more than Paige, the screwup."

"I'm so sorry," she whispered. "I never knew."

I shrugged. "It's in the past. It doesn't matter anymore."

"If it makes you feel any better, I was always jealous of you."

That was news. "You were?"

"Yes." Cammie swirled her spoon around the edge of her ice cream. "Everyone always loved you. You were prettier, smarter. You always got all the attention. And then you grew up to be a famous writer, and all I managed was nothing. I ain't amounted to nothing, Paige. I've had three marriages, no property, nothing that I can call my own. I work a rinky-dink job doing hair. Just what have I accomplished? Nothing. I cain't even afford to go on a real vacation. I'm stuck riding your coattails, hoping you'll take care of me for the next few days. If anyone should be jealous, it's me. You've accomplished so much in your life, and I haven't done one dang thing."

What sort of sister was I that I didn't realize that my own blood was hurting?

I clasped one hand over hers. "From now on I don't want you to feel that way. Everyone has a different path, and if you're jealous because you think I have wealth, don't be. Walter made sure that I was left with nothing, and there wasn't anything when he died, either. So I'm basically starting at zero, and on top of that, I'm middle-aged." I winked. "But don't tell Grim. He thinks I'm a few years younger."

She threw her head back with a laugh. "My sister, the cougar."

I laughed with her, and when our voices settled, our gazes clasped on each other. "Let's be friends."

Cammie squeezed her hand atop mine. "Yes, let's."

CHAPTER 15

*W*hen we finished eating, Cammie said that she had a few errands to do on foot, which I figured meant she wanted to see Ferguson, so we decided to meet a bit later.

I wanted to stretch my legs and walk off some of the ice cream, so I set about some window shopping. I ran into Sanibel, the weaver, while I was out. She had long hair and made the most elaborate tapestries infused with magic.

"How're things?" she asked. "You know, with getting to know your power?"

"It's going okay. Still needs some work."

We were at the farmer's market, and I was picking through the pints of tomatoes, trying to locate the reddest of the bunch. People milled around, but no one was paying attention to us or our conversation.

"You may need to be able to protect yourself, what with the aghash on the loose."

"I'm hoping that was a one-time occurrence."

Sanibel quirked a brow. "How can you be so certain? Often where there's smoke, there's fire."

"I can be certain because…" But I couldn't be, could I? I couldn't be certain of anything. The book was still missing, and another creature could be released from it any time now.

Sanibel seemed to sense my hesitation, because she patted my arm. "Sometimes it's good to be aware. Other times it's best to be prepared."

It wasn't enough to know that the aghash or another creature could be released. I had to take the next step. I had to be ready to fight it.

Man, I hadn't done a thing about studying my powers in days. I spoke to one ghost and could sometimes work magic, but there was certainly no consistency.

When a person was given a gift, they should mold it, shape it, breathe life into it. The only life I'd been breathing was one where I lived to be annoyed by my sister.

Luckily Grim would be teaching me more magic tonight.

I found a pint of beautiful tomatoes and thanked Sanibel for her help. As soon as I was back on the street, Madeleine called.

My heartbeat ticked up. This call would either be great or it would be terrible. With Madeleine, it could go either way.

"Hello?"

"Darling," she purred. "I'm so glad that I caught you."

"You've read what I wrote. Sorry if it was messy. There wasn't time to edit before I sent it to you."

"Well, it is messy," she confirmed. "But nothing that a little comb-over won't fix. Paige, I have to tell you, I was impressed with the first bunch of pages that you sent, but then became worried because I hadn't heard from you in so long. I was afraid that you'd fallen into a slump."

"Me?" I laughed nervously. "No, never. It was just taking some time for the story to brew inside my head."

"As I figured. But anyway, I called to let you know that I love them."

My heart stopped. "You do?"

"I do. They're wonderful. You've outdone yourself. I love the curse and can't wait to see what happens next. Where are you going with it? No. Never mind. Don't tell me. I want to be surprised."

Good. Because I didn't know where I was going, but I knew that thanks to the crystal skull, when I sat down again to write, it would come to me.

"But anyway," she continued, "your editor is going to love it; so will the publisher. You're on the path to redemption, Paige. This work is so different, yet similar enough to your other books that I think your true fans will fall over themselves to read it."

"You think I have any true fans left?"

"Course you do." Her tone chastised me. "You have a legion of fans. They're in hiding now, I'm sure, afraid to admit that they're truly yours. But you have them. They'll buy this book like candy. Just wait and see."

My heart nearly exploded with happiness at the thought that I wasn't completely ruined. Great. Well, at least that was one problem pretty much solved.

Now all I had to do was manage my powers. For some reason it seemed like writing the book might have been easier than learning magic. Or at least controlling my magic.

But one problem at a time, I reminded myself.

When I hung up with Madeleine, I was on cloud nine. She loved what I'd written. That was never a given. In fact, I often lived with crushing self-doubt. I might love a character or a scene, but often readers hated them. When I combed through my reviews (which I knew that I shouldn't, but couldn't help myself), often my attention was glued to the reviewer who couldn't stand a certain choice that I'd made, or the person who believed that my series had run its course and it was time for me to hang up my pen.

Yes, people wrote things like that. People often typed scathing reviews. It was easy, right? No one knew a person's true identity. You could be whoever you wanted on the computer, banging away, crushing someone's dreams with the strike of a key.

But I had thick skin. Sometimes I even agreed with the scorching reviews. Sometimes I didn't. Like with any critic, I took what I needed to and ignored the rest of the noise.

But at that moment, there wasn't any noise. I was all exuberant as I made my way down the street. Realizing that I was only a block away from Dr. Storm's office, I wondered if he was there. It wouldn't hurt to check and let him know how he'd helped open up my mind.

The professor's vehicle was parked on the street. So he was in his office. Bingo! I wouldn't disturb him, at least not for long. All I wanted to do was thank him and leave. That way, if he was catching up on some work, I wouldn't take him away from it for very long.

The corridors were quiet as I made my way to his office. When I arrived outside his door, it was slightly open.

I knocked but no answer came. Perhaps he'd stepped out to the bathroom. I'd go inside and wait. After all, the door was open. That was clearly the universal sign that any and all visitors were welcome.

The front room, which held his desk and visitor chairs, sat empty, but the side room, the one that held the skull, was open.

I tiptoed over to it and murmured, "Dr. Storm?"

Inside the room, there sat a chair facing away from me. Dr. Storm sat in it.

Deciding to forge ahead, I pushed the door and continued. "I just wanted to let you know that what you did last night, using the skull on me, well, it was amazing. I stayed up all night writing, and my agent loved it. She adored every word... Dr. Storm?"

When he didn't respond, I figured that he was asleep. Wanting to make sure that he was all right and grab a blanket for him if he needed it, I stepped around to face him and screamed.

The professor's eyes were wide open, and he stared at the ceiling. His jaw was slack, and a line of drool dripped onto his lapel.

I shook him. "Dr. Storm! Dr. Storm!"

But the professor didn't move. In fact, he continued to stare blindly at the ceiling as if he was either dead...or in a coma.

THE AMBULANCE ARRIVED a few minutes later. The paramedics confirmed that Dr. Storm was alive, which was a relief.

But just like Lulu, he was unresponsive.

I didn't know any of the professor's relatives, so I called Mitch and told him what had happened. I couldn't leave the professor alone with the paramedics. That seemed wrong.

Mitch arrived within minutes. I hugged him and filled him in on what had happened. "I found Dr. Storm in his office a little bit ago. He wasn't responding. I'm not sure if he had a stroke, so I called the paramedics and they're probably going to take him to the ER."

Mitch's brow bent in worry. "First Lulu, now him."

"What do you mean?"

He raked his fingers through his hair. "Oh, nothing. Just seems strange that they've both been unresponsive."

A whimper of sympathy escaped my throat. "The paramedics think it could've been a stroke."

"Yeah." He was lost in thought for a moment before snapping out of it. "But anyway, Paige, thank you for coming and calling me. I've contacted Dr. Storm's wife. She should be on her way."

Mrs. Storm arrived a short time later, as the paramedics were loading the professor into the ambulance. Feeling a bit like a third wheel, I told her that I would be praying for the professor and then left.

I called Grim first thing. "I only went there to thank him, and now he's in the hospital," I said. "I feel so terrible."

"Why?"

"I don't know. It's not my fault that it happened, but he'd been so kind to me yesterday. But Grim"—gosh, just saying his name gave me goose bumps—"what if I somehow called this onto him?"

"I doubt that," he replied in a gravelly tone.

"You don't know that. It's weird. First, you and me find Lulu, and now I discover Dr. Storm."

"Wait."

"What?"

"Do you know for a fact that he was hit with the same ailment that she was?"

"No, I guess not."

"You didn't cause this. This is a coincidence."

"I don't believe in coincidences."

He laughed. "You're starting to sound like me."

I shrugged. "Maybe that's a good thing."

"Look." In the background it sounded like he was scraping food from a pan onto a plate. "I'm going to give you a piece of advice."

"What's that?"

"It's not all about you," he joked.

A laugh burst from my mouth. "You are something, I tell you that. Infuriating and deceptively charming."

"Oh?" I could just picture him quirking a brow. "You think it's charming when I say cutting things?"

"I didn't take it as cutting." I neared a bench and sat on it. "It made me laugh. Thank you."

"For what?"

"For making me feel better."

"Anytime," he told me.

And I felt that he meant it. We secured our plans for that night and I hung up. Cammie and I were supposed to meet in about fifteen minutes, so I had a little time to spare.

Cammie.

My brain started whirling. When I'd told my sister about Professor Storm that morning, she'd murmured that she was angry at him. There had been a good stretch of time between leaving the ice cream shop and finding the professor—a decent stretch.

Theoretically my sister had enough minutes to find the professor's office. If he'd been sitting on his chair like I found him, she could have quietly slipped the gun from her purse and pistol-whipped him until he was knocked unconscious.

But his eyes were open. Was it possible for his eyes to have been open and him be unconscious? Well, if Hollywood movies were any gauge of reality, yes, it was, theoretically.

Oh my goodness. My sister was a maniac. She was going around knocking people into comas.

"You ready to go?" Cammie stood in front of me slurping the last dregs of soda from a cup. "Whew, it's a hot one. I gotta get back to the air-conditioning before I melt."

I eyed her. "What'd you do for the past hour or so?"

She hitched one shoulder to her ear. "Oh, you know. A little bit of this. A little of that."

I nodded. Yep, I knew exactly what little bit Cammie was talking about. I knew it all too well.

CHAPTER 16

Grim was grilling steaks when I arrived. "Haven't I told you that I'm a vegetarian," I joked.

"These are vegan," he said, not missing a beat. "Made from bean paste and carrots."

I retched. "Sounds delightful. Mind if I give mine to your dog?" Savage wagged his tail happily, and I patted his head. "You'd like that, wouldn't you? A bit of bean curd?"

"Okay, okay," Grim said, turning the steaks. "No need to take it that far. He'll get his own bit of steak."

I patted Grim's arm and smiled. "You're such a good dog daddy."

He scowled before his lips turned up into a smile. "Would you like wine? Beer?"

He was drinking a beer, so I decided to match him. "I'll have what you're having."

He handed me one from a cooler beside him. "Nice evening."

It was. The sun was setting, sending pinks and blues smearing the horizon. I'd left Cammie at the house. She was getting ready to have Ferguson pick her up for a date. I trusted that everything would go okay and that she wouldn't attack anyone.

I hoped.

"Penny for your thoughts."

I flashed a smile to Grim. "Don't you think that with inflation, you should be paying me more than a penny?"

"Oh?" He rested the grilling tongs on a plate. "How much were you thinking?"

I pretended to ponder it. "More along the lines of a dime. At least."

He whistled. "Whew. You are an expensive one. You want a dime for your thoughts? Where am I supposed to get all that extra cash?"

I giggled. "You'll figure something out."

"I'm sure that I will," he murmured.

Grim snaked a hand around my waist, and his touch sent a line of fire down to my toes. He bent his head and kissed me gently on the lips. My fingers curled into my fists. They wanted to get wrapped up in his hair, his shirt, his everything, but we were outside and, you know, I had to be responsible.

When we parted, I said, "That was nice."

"There's more where it came from."

"I can't wait to see."

He chuckled. "Come on. Steaks are about done."

He finished grilling and then I helped him bring the rest of the food outside. "Is this homemade potato salad?"

I settled the bowl filled with mayonnaise-covered potatoes on the table.

"It is," he confirmed.

"Why didn't you let me bring anything? I didn't know you were going to this much trouble."

"It's no trouble."

"It is."

He placed a fork atop a napkin and turned to me, his eyes burning with truth. "It's not trouble. I like to cook. I like to create things made from food."

"You also hunt monsters."

"I'm what you call complicated."

I threw my head back and laughed. "You're right. You are complicated. Sensitive enough to cook, yet fierce enough to kill."

"Isn't that what all women want in their lives—a sensitive assassin?"

"I do think you have a point."

We sat and I marveled at the spread that Grim had created—an olive tapenade for the toasted French baguette, the potatoes, a nice green salad filled with artichokes and topped with a raspberry vinaigrette, not to mention the steak.

"Remind me that if I ever need a caterer for any occasion, to call you," I joked.

"It might cost you more than a dime," he volleyed back.

"I would expect it to."

"Here. Have you tried this?" He topped a slice of sweet garlic pickle with a small hunk of cheese. "It's amazing."

I tried not to grimace. "A pickle and cheese?"

"Yes." His eyes teased me. "You'll love it."

I wasn't sure if that was true, but I did try it. The sweet and spicy tang of the pickle mingled with the cool, creamy cheese. It was…divine.

"Oh my goodness, that is so good. Forget the steak, I want cheese and pickles."

Grim laughed. "Don't worry, there's more."

I ate everything in sight and had to undo the top button of my jeans by the time I was finished gorging on the meal that Grim had created.

When we were washing up, I told him, "You outdid yourself. You didn't have to do all that for me."

"Yes, I did." He rinsed a plate and handed it to me for wiping. "I wanted you to know how I feel about you."

"That you want to make me fat?" I teased.

"No. That I like you."

A smattering of red tinged his cheeks and probably did the same to mine. I bit back the smile that threatened to take over my entire face.

"Well, I like you, too," I told him.

He smiled that perfect one-thousand-watt smile that made the corners of his silver eyes crinkle. The whole way his face morphed into sheer happiness made my heart go all soft and squishy.

I was really a sap for this guy.

He poured us each a glass of wine, and we headed into the living room, where Savage slapped his tail against the floor but made no move to get out of his bed by the fireplace.

"He's a good dog," I said.

Grim nodded. "He is."

He sat on the couch, and I sat beside him a few feet away so that I could angle myself to face him, knee up on the cushion.

"So," I started.

"So," he replied, amusement tinging his voice. "I assume at this point in the night you want to know all my secrets."

"Is that what time it is?" I jokingly checked my watch. "Oh, sure is. It's time to play skeletons in the closet. What ones do you have?"

He laughed. "You first."

"Okay, well, my sister is visiting."

"That's not much of a skeleton."

"Au contraire, mon frère. You do not know my sister."

He sipped his wine and chuckled. "All right then, you win for most scary skeleton."

He wasn't getting off the hook that easily. But I also didn't want to push Grim. If he wanted to reveal his darkest, scariest secrets, so be it. It wouldn't do to twist his arm into it.

So I started talking, telling him more about Walter, about how we'd been so in love at first and admitting that over the years the relationship dragged and sagged. I got busy. He did, too.

"I should've put more effort into it. You get out what you put in, right? But when I discovered that he'd peeped on our neighbor, that just about did me in."

Grim studied me with curious eyes. "Peeped as in Tom-like behavior?"

"Exactly that. He spied on her undressing."

"Well, Walter was a fool, because he had a beautiful woman at home."

My heart swelled to the size of a beach ball. "Thank you for saying that."

"It's true," he said fiercely. "We don't know each other well, but I know that you're a good person. I was in a relationship once with a woman. Well, let me backtrack. I *thought* she was a woman."

That was an unexpected twist. "What do you mean, you *thought* she was?"

He drained the last swallow of wine from his glass and settled it on the table. "Just that. Looked like a woman. Smelled like one, too. We met and she was nothing like anyone I'd ever met."

A twinge of jealousy pricked my heart. *I* was supposed to be unlike any woman he'd ever met. But in reality when you'd lived awhile, it was unreasonable to think that you were the most interesting person your new man had ever met.

But instead of getting all silly, I asked, "How was she different?"

"She improvised life. If Daria wanted to spend a weekend in New York, she just went. She didn't plan much, and that was very intriguing. Me, I'm a planner. I think things through methodically. It's part of my job. If I'm careless, it could cost me my life, or someone else their life."

"Makes sense," I only said, waiting for him to continue.

Which he did. "At first I thought Daria was everything that I'd ever been looking for. She was beautiful and sensitive, always seeming to know my mood before I did."

Wow. That was going to be fun to live up to. Did Grim realize that he was killing my ego one word at a time? But even though his description of Daria was chiseling away at my confidence, I just kept right on smiling, as if it didn't matter, as if I were made of stone and not Silly Putty.

"But then things changed," Grim told me. "Daria became moody. She stopped being so impromptu and only wanted to stay where she was. What I didn't realize at the time was that she was getting hungry."

"Hungry? Or hangry?"

"Both," he said darkly. "Daria had a secret, one that I didn't catch until it was too late."

He paused and I wasn't sure if he wanted me to ask the next question or not, so I just went for it. "What secret did she hold?"

"She was a *lamia*, a monster."

"What's a lamia?"

He scrubbed his palm down his face. "It's a creature that looks like a woman but preys on children."

"Oh my word."

He nodded. "I didn't catch it until it was almost too late. One night I had the sense that a monster was near. I could smell the evil desire within it, almost like it was sweating from its pores its want to kill. I followed the scent to a house, and there I found Daria creeping outside.

"I confronted her and she turned toward me with fangs and talons. I quickly realized that she'd come to our town sated and full. When Daria would travel out on the weekends, she was filling her need to devour. That's why I was never clued in to what she really was. We fought and she managed to set a fire and torched my back."

"The scar," I murmured.

He nodded. "It's there, a reminder to be careful who I trust."

"And Daria?"

Grim shook his head. "I defeated her. Never in my life have I been more thankful for what I was than that night. I only wished that I'd seen her for what she was earlier. If so, others could've been saved."

I squeezed his hand. "You got her in the end. That's what matters."

He took my hand and pressed the inside of my palm to his lips. "The hands of time can never be unwound. We can only move forward and pray that our choices are the right ones."

My heart ached at his pain. "I'm sorry for what you went through."

He released my hand. "You live and learn, right? And I guess the one lesson that I took away from that night was that it was best not to get too attached. It's a promise I've kept a long time."

My heart shriveled to the size of a pea. "Right. That makes total sense. I can see that."

Great. So Grim had just admitted that he didn't want anything serious. So where did that put me?

I settled my glass on the table. "So. How about those magic lessons?"

His eyes narrowed in confusion and then he rose. "Right. Let's go outside."

"Yes," I replied, following him out the door as my heart slowly cracked into a thousand pieces, "let's."

CHAPTER 17

"How am I supposed to summon my magic if I can only take on the powers of the witch or wizard that I'm around?"

"Good question," Grim said. "*Very* good question, and one that it took my mother a long time to figure out."

The frogs and crickets chirped loudly. Grim had ignited some tiki lights. Those, along with floodlights attached to his house gave us enough light to see by.

"What did she learn?" I asked.

"I don't know. She died before telling me."

My heart lurched. There was way too much heart lurching going on this night. First, I'd learned that basically Grim would never love again. All right, maybe he hadn't said that directly, but he'd *implied* it.

Now I'd been stupid enough to bring up his dead mother. I was really batting low. Or high. Whatever the saying about batting meant.

Perhaps I was simply striking out.

"I have an idea," Grim told me.

That piqued my interest. "About my powers?"

"That's the one."

"And it is?"

He moved around me in a semicircle, like we were in a battling ring instead of standing in his backyard. "If you've come in contact with a power, I believe that you can access it always."

"How?"

"By using your mind and remembering what it felt like to have that magic."

"I like that idea." How cool would that be? No matter what sort of witch or wizard I was facing off against (and I was giving myself a lot of credit that a witch or wizard wanted to fight me), I could conjure a power I'd used before. "We should start simply."

Grim clapped his hands, rearing to go. "Good. What ability do you want to use—and not mine, since we've already been in contact this evening."

"How about the power of vegetation."

He quirked a brow. "Vegetation?"

"I don't know what it's called," I told him, frustration lacing my voice. "But it's what Estelle Butts has—she can use vines and crap, control the grass."

He cracked his knuckles. "The power of vegetation it is."

I glared at him. "Are you making fun of me?"

"Absolutely not. To be perfectly honest, I don't know what it's called, either."

"But you have an idea."

"I might." He cocked his jaw. "But I like the power of vegetation. It has a nice ring to it."

"So what do I do?"

"Summon it." He gestured to me. "From the depths of your mind."

"If only I had a crystal skull," I joked. "Then maybe I'd get some-where a lot faster."

"Last I heard, Professor Storm was in a coma."

"He is?" I clutched my stomach to stop the knots forming in it. "You sure?"

"Just like Lulu."

"What is Ferguson doing about it? I saw a flyer, but is there anything else happening?"

"Everyone is on alert. They know about the aghash. But whatever this is, it's not that creature."

No, it wasn't. But what was causing the comas? "Perhaps it's a different monster from the book?"

"I'm not sure." He clapped his hands. "But back to you and this power. Try it."

I did my best to tap into it, focusing on a few blades of grass at my feet. Maybe they'd grow if I focused hard enough. I gritted my teeth and strained, trying to coax my power out.

And wouldn't you know it, but I swore that the blades extended an inch. That was victory enough for me. I threw my hands up and rushed over to Grim, embracing him.

"I did it! I made grass grow!"

"I know. I saw it!"

And then his hand was on my head and my fingers were running up his back, doing my best to avoid the tender scar that was lashed over his flesh. Then they were winding through his hair, and his lips were on my cheek, my jaw, my mouth.

And my lips were parting, and fireworks were exploding in my body. Buttons were being frantically undone and we were lying on the grass and his words about Daria and how she was the best thing in the entire world and he'd never give himself over to another woman ever again flitted in my head, but I didn't care.

But I was supposed to. Hadn't I literally just five seconds earlier decided that I wouldn't do this? That I wouldn't go crazy with him even though I was technically middle-aged and who cared about consequences?

Well, my heart cared, and it would be broken when Grim was finished and everything between us was over.

"Wait." I pressed a hand to his burning-hot chest that was naked and totally amazing. "Slow down."

He sat up. "Sorry. I lost control of myself."

He helped me sit up, and I redid the buttons on my shirt. "It's been a great night. It's just…it's nothing personal."

He smiled tenderly. "It's fine. We don't know each other that well."

"Right." Our gazes locked and I felt myself falling down the well of Grim. If I didn't come out now, I'd be lost forever. "But hey, grass grown. So cool."

He chuckled. "Very cool." We were silent for a moment before he said, "Is something bothering you?"

"No, why?"

"You just seem a little off, is all."

Well, I was trying to avoid my heart getting broken. "There's a good reason for that. I think that—this sounds crazy, I know. But I think that my sister might be behind the attacks."

"And what makes you say that?"

I couldn't tell by Grim's expression if he thought that I was crazy or…he thought that I was crazy. But it didn't matter. I knew what I knew.

I brushed grass from the backs of my legs. "She's got a gun."

He paused and scratched his chin. "But no one was shot."

"I'm going with, they were pistol-whipped." He coughed into his hand. But it looked suspiciously like he was hiding a laugh. "You think that I'm crazy, don't you?"

"No, of course not. It's just that I don't see the connection between your sister and the victims."

"Oh, that part I can convince you of. First, she had an argument with Lulu at the library."

"The library?" he asked doubtfully.

"Yes."

"Not a place that I consider a hub of conflict."

"Me neither, but it happened. They got into an argument over a book. And with the professor, Cammie wanted revenge because he ruined her date with Ferguson. You see, when he melded my mind with the crystal skull, the professor gave me all these ideas, and I barged in on Cammie and Ferguson. They were…well, you know. I mean, not quite there, but close."

He rose and took my hand, giving me a lift up. "And because of this you think that she attacked Dr. Storm?"

"Cammie was very angry that her date got ruined, and we'd left each other for a while yesterday. She had time to go to his office, pistol-whip him and meet up with me later." I smiled brightly. "See? Case solved."

"Yeah, case solved," he said, sounding amused.

"You don't believe me."

He flinched. "It's not that I don't believe you; it's that it doesn't seem likely that she's the person or thing behind all of this."

"Lulu had a bump on the back of her head," I reminded him.

"Yes," Grim replied slowly, seeming to search for the right words, "but I don't know it's likely two people could be pistol-whipped and both end up in comas."

He had a point. But there was still something suspicious going on with Cammie. I'd noticed that the other night at the restaurant. She'd looked nervous. Plus, she had the gun.

"I still think there's something there," I told him.

Grim shrugged. "Maybe." He glanced out into the darkness. "It's getting late."

A yawn escaped my mouth before I could stop it. "You're right. I should be going."

"I'd drive you, but you drove yourself here, and to be honest, I didn't know when you'd be leaving."

A pang of regret tightened my chest. I'd wanted nothing more than to throw off my clothes and roll around with Grim, but I just couldn't shake the fact that he was still tethered to the past. He'd said that he'd learned the lesson of not getting too attached. If that was the case, I didn't want to get too attached, either.

"I had a nice time," I told him as I followed him to the gate.

He reached back and took my hand, and warmth flowed through me. Oh gosh, even if he didn't want to get too attached, I wanted to hold his hand forever. We reached the gate, and he walked through it, still holding my hand.

We stood in front of my car, and he glanced down at me with smoldering eyes. His fingers were lacing around mine now. He was leaning on his right hip, and it was touching me. I stared up at him and didn't want this night to end. I could die just touching him. That would be enough, I thought. He didn't have to become emotionally attached, just sort of physically attached to me and I'd be good.

His phone vibrated in his pocket, lighting up his pants. He didn't stop holding my hand and I didn't stop enjoying how warm he was as it went to voice mail.

"I had a great night," he told me.

I started to tell him the same when his phone rang again. "Must be important," I said.

Grim kept holding my hand as he retrieved his phone. "It's Cowan. Hold on." He thumbed the screen to life. "This is Grim." His fingers traced mine down to the tips and back as he talked. "What? How many?"

Pause. He adjusted his stance, and his hip pressed harder against me. His body was a wall of heat. His temperature, along with the summer humidity, made sweat sprout on my upper lip. I wiped it away before Grim had a chance to see it.

"Are you sure?" He scowled. "I'll be right there."

As soon as he hung up, I said, "What happened?"

He stared at his phone as if it had caused the problem before sliding it back into his pocket. "There are more victims."

"More?"

He nodded. "Twenty more. People who are all in comas."

My jaw dropped. "What?"

"There are so many of them that the hospital is having to clear out the ER to source beds. This isn't the work of your sister. Cowan is also convinced it's magical." He smiled tightly. "Let's get you home."

"And what about you?"

"I'm going down to the hospital to see if there's anything that I can do."

I squeezed his hand. "If that's what you're doing, I'm doing it, too. You're not going anywhere without me."

Grim smiled. "Come on. Let's get out of here and find out what's attacking people."

CHAPTER 18

The ER was bursting with full beds when we arrived. People were even lying on gurneys lining the halls. The place looked like a war zone.

I was definitely out of my element and had no problem letting Grim take the lead.

Cowan greeted him and then me. "Ms. Provey, I'd like to say it's nice to see you, but as you can tell, we've got a situation on our hands."

"I won't get in the way," I assured him, standing a bit behind Grim but keeping my body close to his. Ever since we'd left his house, some body part of ours had been touching the other person's. On the bike ride over, I had my arms hugged around him. When we walked across the parking lot, our hands were beside one another's, our skin brushing. When we'd walked in the door, Grim had kept his strides short, telling me to stay close and making sure that his arm was against mine the whole way.

I had the feeling that I wouldn't like it when we stopped touching. But that was a problem for another situation.

"What happened?" Grim asked.

Cowan scratched his head. "All I know is that I got a call from the ER explaining that an influx of folks had been discovered comatose and that I'd better get down here fast."

"Poisoning?" Grim asked.

"Not as far as we know." Cowan placed his hands on his hips and moved in close. "It's strange, Grim. No one can explain it, not the doctors—nobody. It's beginning to make me wonder if there's something in the water, and if I should warn folks not to drink it."

"Let me take a look," he said.

"I told a doc you might be coming." Cowan signaled to one of the doctors, a man in a white coat, and he nodded. "All right. We've got clearance. There's a victim I want you to see."

Cowan escorted us to a room in the ER. A sliding glass door separated the chamber from the larger anteroom, where the nurses' computer stations were organized into a wall facing the patients so that they could look in on them at any time.

Cowan told the nurse we were going in. He slid the door open and we stepped inside.

The man lying on the bed was young, perhaps early twenties, with his hair clipped short on the sides and with a thick patch of soft fuzz in the middle, like a grown-out mohawk. He was much too young to have been lying in a hospital bed attached to machines and a nutrition drip that fed into his veins.

"He was the first to be found," Cowan said. "And it's because of his short hair that we found this."

He gently tipped the man's face to the left, and behind his right ear, just inside a patch of hair, was a triangle with a swirl in the middle of it. The symbol looked so familiar, but I couldn't quite place where I'd seen it before.

"Do you recognize it?" he asked Grim.

Grim shook his head. "No. I'm not familiar with it."

Cowan's expression fell. "It's the first solid lead we have in this. The victim lives with his parents, and when I asked them about the symbol, they said it was brand-new. Their son hadn't had it earlier in the day."

Grim leaned down and inspected it. "That's not a tattoo."

"No, and we've already checked with all the local shops. This guy didn't get ink today."

Grim pressed his thumb lightly to the mark. "It's magic," he said, surprise tinging his voice.

Cowan's eyes narrowed as he bent over to get a better look at the mark. "Magic? Do you recognize it?"

Grim shook his head. "It's nothing like I've seen before. I don't know of any creature that leaves a person in a coma and also brands a victim. Because it's usually in the killing that the person is marked."

"I see," Cowan said.

"The population needs to be made aware. They need to know that a creature could be on the loose, sucking them of their life energy."

"And how do you expect me to explain that to the vacationing population of Willow Lake? To all the humans out there? You want me to tell them that something's feeding on them?"

"I don't care what you tell them," Grim said sharply. "All I care about is the safety of the community. This is about them, not about us or our reputations."

"You'll have to close the lake," I muttered.

"What?" Cowan said with a scowl.

"To keep people away, you'll have to close the lake."

The officer shook his head. "And how am I supposed to do that?"

"She's right," Grim told him. "If you want to keep people safe, tell them the lake's off-limits. They'll leave, which will minimize the risk of attack."

"And what about the rest of the population?" he asked. "What am I supposed to tell them?"

Grim considered it before saying, "Send some of your men to the lake in hazmat suits. Tell people to limit trips out and about town until we have the answer. Once we catch whoever or whatever is doing this, it's back to business."

"I'm going to have the city council all over my back," Cowan complained. "The mayor's not going to take this well."

Fire burned in Grim's eyes. "Then tell the mayor to call me. He can deal with me directly."

"I don't like it, Grim," Cowan replied with a shake of his head.

"It's not about liking it. Now. I've got some research to do." He took my hand, and we left Cowan alone to figure out how to appease the mayor and the city council, all while keeping the good people of Willow Lake safe.

GRIM DROPPED me off at my house, told me that he didn't want me driving by myself home. I pointed out that he would be doing the same after leaving me. He only grunted in response.

When I got inside, I found Cammie asleep on the couch. Well, I guessed she wasn't our criminal after all. She was only my gun-toting sister, intent on having a leprechaun for a boyfriend.

I quietly washed my face and brushed my teeth before heading into my bedroom. Once I slipped under the covers, worry started to settle in. What if Grim didn't make it home okay? I texted him to tell me when he got home, and while waiting for that, I thought about that symbol on the man's head.

I'd seen it before. That, I knew. But where? Doggone it. Why couldn't I remember? Probably because I'd suffered the emotional trauma of having my sister visit.

My phone chimed. Grim had replied. He'd made it home, sending a heart at the end of the message.

Oh crap. I was never good with emojis. Was I supposed to send a heart back or a kissy-face? Or a thumbs up? Definitely not a thumbs-up or an eggplant. I might not have known much, but I knew that an eggplant was the universal sign for a certain male body part.

I put a heart into the conversation box, and it was huge, like stalker-girl huge. Oh no, that had to be deleted. Realizing that Grim was probably seeing my text bubbles, I needed to do something fast, so I simply typed out *good night* and added a heart. There. The heart didn't look like it wanted to eat him.

Perfect.

I slipped the phone onto my nightstand and closed my eyes. Next thing I knew, the windows were bright and I was up, awake. There were sounds coming from the bathroom, which must've been Cammie, so I knocked on the door.

"Boy, am I glad you're here. There's some craziness going on in town."

Sounded like the hair dryer had kicked on. She spoke over it. "Oh, there is?"

"Yes." I started to make myself a cup of coffee and called out to her in the process. "People are winding up in comas. It's not good. We don't need to go into town alone until this whole thing is figured out. I mean, I went to the ER last night, and it was full of people. There were even gurneys in the hall."

"You don't say," she called.

"That's a fact." My coffee finished dripping, and I added cream to it and took it over to the table. "We should probably not have Abe deliver anything, either. I wouldn't want anything to happen to him."

"Me neither."

"Good. Glad we're on the same page."

I opened my laptop and scrolled through the daily news, which was mostly depressing, so I opted for the celebrity highlights, which weren't nearly as heavy—mostly about cosmetic butt jobs and who was in trouble for speaking the truth about certain topics.

But the butt job thing was interesting. Perhaps I should consider one. Once I finished my book, that was, and I had extra money for such a thing.

I finished my coffee, and the hair blower was still on. How long did it take Cammie to dry her locks? "You okay in there?"

"Oh yeah, I'm fine."

"Did you have a good night?"

"Sure did."

Of course she did. Cammie had probably gotten some. She wasn't the sort to be worried about a man who didn't want to be attached. She'd just say, to heck with it, and knock knees with him anyway.

"How was Ferguson?" I asked.

The hair dryer switched off and the door opened. Snow's head popped out. "Who?"

I shrieked from being startled. "I thought you were Cammie!"

"No, I'm just me."

Accusation filled my voice. "What were you doing in there with the hair dryer on? You don't have anything to dry."

"I just like to relive the old days," she explained brightly. "It makes me feel good to turn on the blower and let the air run through my hair."

I shook my head in frustration. "But it doesn't even move your hair because that doesn't exist as a tangible thing."

Snow smiled wistfully. "A girl can pretend, can't she?"

I just…I couldn't deal with that. "Where's Cammie? I thought that it was her I was talking to."

"Oh, Cammie? She left an hour ago. I didn't catch where she was going as she can't see me, so she doesn't talk to me."

Oh no. I rushed into my room and threw open my drawers, pulling out jeans and a T-shirt.

"This is bad," I moaned. "Terrible. We've got to find her?"

"Why?"

"Because." I whirled on Snow, who looked as terrified as I felt. "There's a creature on the loose in this town, and I'm afraid Cammie could be its next victim."

CHAPTER 19

*T*he only problem with me dashing into town was the fact that I was currently carless. I hated to call Grim so early because it looked rather desperate, like I wanted to spend time with him (which I did, but he didn't need to know that because, you know, dating games), but there was no other choice.

"I need my car," I told him. "Cammie's gone into town, and I haven't had a chance to tell her to steer clear."

"I'll be right there."

While I waited, I called my sister to see if I could track her down. I dialed the number, but it went straight to voice mail. Crap. There was no telling if she'd turned it off, it was drained of battery life or if she saw that I was calling and hit the snooze button.

Lucky for me, Grim didn't take long. In fact, he arrived driving my car and with a police cruiser behind him. "I called in a favor," he explained when he saw the questioning look on my face. "I knew you wouldn't want to waste time."

"Thank you." I squeezed his solid bicep and nearly fainted. "I appreciate it."

He smiled and handed me the keys. "You're welcome. The police have their hands busy closing down the lake. Folks are giving them a hard time."

Summer was the busy season, so I wasn't surprised. "Hopefully we'll figure out what's behind all of this and the lake will reopen quickly."

He nodded hard. "I'm going out to help them. Cowan phoned me a little bit ago. Otherwise, I'd help you find Cammie."

"It's okay."

"But if anything happens, anything at all, and you need me, don't hesitate to call."

"Thank you."

With that, Grim got into the cruiser with the officer and they left. I felt very alone. I didn't know where Cammie was, and Grim couldn't help me. I had to fend for myself in this new world of magic and mayhem.

Snow, who'd been hovering nearby, approached. "I'll go with you. It never hurts to have an extra set of eyes when you're looking for someone."

"Thank you."

Traffic was thick heading out of town. It reminded me of a disaster movie, when people are attempting to flee a city because of aliens or a looming volcanic eruption.

There wasn't a roadblock into town, which was opposite of what I'd expected. For now, most of the police were probably at entrance roads to the lake, explaining that people needed to evacuate.

Town was so quiet when we entered that it wouldn't have surprised me if a tumbleweed rolled across the road.

"Wow, it's like the place is abandoned," Snow said.

"It's only for a few days. Hopefully Grim and Cowan will figure out what's behind putting people into comas and everything will be as it was." I scanned the sidewalks. "Now. Let's find Cammie."

A few shops were open, but from what I could see, there weren't people inside. Okay. The only way to find Cammie would be to get inside of her head. If I was my sister, where would I be at nine a.m. on a Saturday? I would either be at a pharmacy or at the grocery store.

Grocery store! She was probably picking up more items for her and Ferguson. I parked at Werewolf Grocery, which was Wilson's Grocery to folks who weren't magical.

Cammie's car was parked in a spot by the front door. "Aha! She's here!"

"Oh good," Snow said. "I'll come in with you. Sometimes this place is full of spirits."

I frowned. "At the grocery store?"

She rolled her eyes. "You'd be surprised where ghosts like to hang out. Before the new owners bought it, the place had a cafe inside where you could order a coffee and biscuit. Lots of folks would meet up for breakfast."

Ah, right. That whole old folks daily routine—meet up for coffee at Jack's restaurant. That was a chain burger joint in the South. I'd witnessed it plenty of times in my day.

"That's fine," I told her. "Let's get in there and grab my sister."

I'd been in Werewolf Grocery several times. But maybe because people were being forced from town, or maybe because Snow had just made me aware of it, on this visit I noticed that she wasn't kidding about the ghosts. There were spirits hanging out everywhere, and they were eyeing me as if I was the answer to all their problems.

"She's mine," Cammie told them possessively. "She's trying to help me figure out who put me in a book, so y'all can't have her."

A plan that I'd really let fall by the wayside. With Cammie's appearance, I'd completely forgotten about the mystery surrounding Snow's death.

But back to the scene. Spirits milled about and it was hard not to stare. They looked like regular people out and about, if they were dressed a bit out of fashion—like in bell bottoms or a dress that went all the way to the throat with ruffles at the neck and wrists. So yes, the folks lingering in the store ran the gamut from the seventies to the eighties and all the way to the nineties when Snow was killed.

My gaze landed on Cammie immediately. She stood at the checkout counter with swath of food on the belt wine and cheese, expensive smoked meats, crackers, nuts and fruit.

"Thank goodness I found you," I exclaimed.

Cammie jumped at my voice. She clutched her neck, and when her eyes snapped on mine, she relaxed. "Paige, you just about scared me to death."

"Sorry, but I've been looking for you."

We talked while the cashier swiped food over the scanner. A soft *beep* filled the gaps in our sentences.

"What for?" She tapped her foot impatiently. Or was that nervousness. Cammie's gaze was swinging around again. She was on edge about something. "Why would you be looking for me?"

"Because there's something going on at the lake. The police have closed it. I think it was a chemical spill or something. They want nonessential workers to stay home."

She shrugged. "Well, we need food."

"This isn't food. This is entertainment fare."

"Potato, *pahtahto*," she joked.

The cashier, whose face was covered in soft fur, finished ringing up the last item. "That'll be one hundred fifty dollars and twenty-three cents."

"Whew, that inflation is sure turning out to be something," Cammie griped. "So bad. But anyway, Paige, why don't you go on outside, and I'll finish up here and meet you at the car."

"No, I'll wait."

Cammie smiled tightly. "You don't have to."

"It's okay."

"How would you like to pay?" the cashier asked. "Debit or cash."

"It'll be credit." Cammie turned away from me and pulled a card from her purse. She shoved it toward the cashier, who tapped a small box in front of her. "Swipe it in there, please."

Cammie's lips tightened. "Sure." She shoved the card into the machine, putting her back to me while she did so. When the card was approved, she pulled it out and I caught a flash of blue.

"Cammie, is that my card?"

She tossed it into her purse. "Don't be silly. Of course not."

"Then let me see it."

"Oops, it's been swallowed by the black hole that's my bag." She shouldered the purse. "I'll let you see it later, when we get home."

"Now." I opened my palm. "I want to see it right now."

My sister reluctantly opened her bag and retrieved the card, slapping it into my hand. "It's no big deal. I'll pay you back."

But it was a big deal. As I held the card, *my* credit card, the one that my sister had swiped from my own purse, fury buzzed in my veins.

This was a big deal because I was living on a tight budget. I went out to eat some but not very much. I watched what I spent because I was currently living off my savings, or what was left of it. The fact that my sister was draining what little money I had left, dry, and running up a big bill was infuriating.

"Cammie, you had no right—"

"Let's talk about this outside." Her gaze flitted to the cashier, who was bagging up the groceries. "You know, in private."

"No," I said coldly, "let's discuss this now."

"Uh-oh," Snow said. "You need to calm it down. All your anger is making them upset, too."

I glanced over to see what she was talking about. The spirits, the ones who'd been mostly minding their own business, were coming toward us.

I didn't care. What were they going to do? Pick up a grocery bag?

"Cammie, you had no right to do that," I snapped. "I'm basically broke. I can't afford — what is this?" I snatched a hunk of cheese from a sack. "I can't afford Murray's smoked cheddar cheese. My God! It's twenty dollars for a quarter of a pound. What's it made of, gold?"

"It's aged." Cammie yanked the cheese from me and tossed it back into the bag. "Look. Like I said, I'll pay you. Can we just go."

"No, we cannot go," I screeched. "You will pay me right now, with whatever you've got in your purse."

I grabbed her bag, but Cammie held tight. "Let it go," she yelled.

But I wasn't about to. I'd seen some cash in her wallet before. I wanted all of it, every last dime. I dipped my hand in, but she pulled hard in the opposite direction. I was not about to let my sister win, so I dug my fingers in and yanked with all my might.

"Give it to me!"

My burst of strength took Cammie by surprise. It took me by surprise, too. I pulled so hard that she let go and the bag's contents flew from the opening. Her wallet (along with a pen and lipstick) landed with a thud on the skid-mark-laden linoleum floor.

I was about to reach for it when the spirit in bell bottoms picked up the wallet and brought it to me.

"What in the world?" Cammie whispered.

The ghost held the wallet out to me, and not wanting to be rude, I said, "Thank you."

That was when Cammie murmured, "Oh my goodness, Paige. I didn't know."

I scoffed, annoyed that she was even speaking. "Didn't know what?"

Her hand touched my shoulder. "That you could communicate with spirits."

CHAPTER 20

Cammie not seeming surprised back in the grocery store that I could communicate with spirits had shaken me to the core. So much that I'd pushed aside her swiping my credit card so that we could get home and talk.

But that didn't mean I'd forgiven her for snatching it.

We'd each driven home individually, and when we arrived, I helped Cammie unpack *my* groceries—none of which, I had decided that anyone would be eating outside of the house. Ferguson had a job. If he wanted to eat deli meat and smoked cheese, he could buy his own. For now I'd savor at least one bite of every package that Cammie had purchased.

"So," she started.

"Not until I'm ready," I told her.

"Someone sure is grumpy," Snow remarked.

I shot her a scathing look and set about creating a platter of delights to snack from. I sliced apples and added cheese and crackers, a dollop of mustard and toasted some sourdough and put it all together.

I took the platter to the table and sat across from Cammie. When she reached for a cracker, I pulled the plate closer.

"It's all mine."

She looked wounded, but I didn't care. I was hangry and…more hangry. "So," I said after I'd taken several bites of a smoky cheese with an aroma that bloomed in my mouth, "you didn't seem surprised when you saw that I can communicate with spirits."

Cammie inspected her manicure for a moment before answering. "I wasn't. Maw Maw Taylor could see things."

That was news to me. "She could?"

"Yeah. You don't remember because you were too little. But sometimes she'd tell me that her spirit friends were near."

"Spirit friends?"

"They guided her and helped with things." Cammie's face softened wistfully. "She made it seem like the ghosts were no big deal, that they were a part of life, always around. She told me that one day I might be able to see them, too, and I always thought that I could. I wanted to. But as you can see, I don't have any such gift like you do."

I was so confused. "So she had the gift?"

"Yeah. What aren't you wrapping your head around?"

I nibbled on the snack while I spoke. "Well, for one, I'm confused because I couldn't see anything until I showed up here and was hit on the head by a falling book."

"A falling book?"

I waved away her question. "It's complicated. I've only recently been touched with this ability. If Maw Maw Taylor had it, why didn't I get it earlier?"

Cammie shrugged. "She told me once that the gift would present itself when the time was right."

Okay, so maybe the time had just been right. But what about the magical abilities? "As far as you know, could she, Maw Maw, could she do anything else?"

"What do you mean?"

I pushed the plate toward Cammie, and she grabbed a mound of apple slices and started chomping on them. "I mean, did she, I don't know, talk about spells or anything like that."

"You mean, did she shoot lasers from her fingers?"

Yes. "No. That's ridiculous. Nothing like that. That's not even a possibility," I added with a nervous laugh. "Just did she have any other abilities that you remember?"

Cammie shook her head. "No. That was it. That was all she could do. But I think that's enough, don't you? I mean, being able to talk to spirits is pretty cool." Her eyes sparkled. "You are pretty cool, sis. You can talk to spirits. What do they tell you? Can you see the future? What do you see for me? Wait. Don't tell me. I want to be surprised." Her gaze darted around. "Is there one in this room?"

"Yes."

Cammie bolted straight up. "There is?"

"Yes. Her name's Snow."

"Tell her that I'm trying to find out who murdered me," the spirit prodded.

"And Snow is trying to discover who killed her."

Cammie clutched her chest. "You mean, it's a mystery and she needs you to help her solve it? Oh my gosh. This is like so many books I've read." She splayed her arms out. "The ghost appears to a medium and explains that they've been murdered by someone and they need help solving the mystery. This is so exciting!"

Cammie jumped up and grabbed a notebook and pencil from the counter. "What are you doing?" I asked.

"I'm writing down all the clues so that we can help Snow. She needs us, Paige. I mean, have you helped her at all?"

My stomach knotted. "Um, well, no. But I've been busy with other things."

My sister pointed the pencil at me accusingly. "Just what kind of friend are you that you haven't helped this poor woman yet? Time's a'wasting. We'd best get on it. Now. Tell me everything that you know."

Snow crossed to us and sat at an empty chair between us. She considered her words carefully as she spoke. "Well, I know that my next-door neighbor was Pam. That's really all that I can say."

I told Cammie this, and she said, "Does she think Pam still lives in the area?"

"I'm not sure," Snow replied.

"Can she remember where she lived?" Cammie asked.

Snow said that she could.

"And what were you doing the day that you were murdered?" my sister said.

Snow replied, "I was doing laundry. The baby was asleep. Oh my gosh!" Her hands flew to her face. "The baby! How could I have forgotten? Paige, I had a baby. And a husband. Where are they? What happened to them? I can't remember even my last name. I can barely recall my husband's face. His name was…I don't know."

"We'll find out," I told her soothingly. I explained to Cammie what Snow had said, and my sister jumped to her feet. "What are we waiting for? Let's ride around town and find out where she lived and who this Pam is and everything."

"We can't," I told her. "The town's on lockdown. That's why I came to find you. There's been some sort of something that happened at the lake."

She frowned. "What sort of something?"

"I'm not sure, but they've closed the water. No one can go out there, and they don't want people roaming about town."

"But this isn't roaming," Cammie argued. "This is research. We'll only be driving. It's not like we're gonna get out or anything. What's the worst that could happen?"

Not wanting to go down that path, I said, "Maybe we should stay here."

"You can. But I'm not."

I rose and crossed my arms in warning. "May I remind you that you stole my credit card. *Stole it.* Why would you do such a thing?"

"I'm so sorry."

"Sorry isn't good enough. I need an explanation. You have cash. I've seen you use it."

Cammie bit her bottom lip. "The truth is that I don't have much cash, and I was afraid of it running out before I left."

I slapped my thigh in frustration. "Why didn't you just tell me that?"

"Because I was embarrassed. It isn't fun or easy to tell your little sister that you need her help. I'm sorry that I did it, that I used your card. Here." She opened her purse and pulled out a handful of cash. "Take it. It should be more than what I owe you."

She'd handed me a crumpled mound of twenties and hundred-dollar bills. "Listen, I don't want your money. I just want you to be honest. If you need to keep the cash, keep it. I'll be fine. Just don't use my credit card again."

"I won't," she promised. "And for what it's worth, I'm sorry, Paige."

"It's okay," I replied, feeling myself soften. "It'll be fine."

"All right, then." Cammie grabbed her keys and headed toward the door. "You coming?"

"Where are we going, again?"

"To find out about Snow—her old neighbor and see if this Pam is still living there."

"But the lockdown."

She smirked. "Now, Paige. Since when did you let a little lockdown get in the way of fun?"

"It really isn't safe."

"Neither is life. You can live indoors and be safe, or go exploring and have an adventure." She twisted the door handle. "So. Do you want to have fun or be safe?"

Well, when she put it that way… "Let me just grab my purse."

THE NEIGHBORHOODS WERE quiet as we slipped through town. "Boy, this sure is eerie," Cammie murmured.

"It's very strange," Snow agreed.

I didn't like being the only car on the road. It made me feel exposed. I just hoped the police were too busy at the lake to patrol town, because by the time we arrived back in the center of it, signs had been posted telling folks to stay home for the time being.

I didn't exactly want to encounter whatever was putting people into comas with my sister and a ghost. I didn't think that the three of us would stand a fighting chance against the thing.

But Grim was on the case, and if anyone could figure out what was behind this, he could.

Snow quickly remembered exactly where she'd lived before. The neighborhood was quiet and well-kept. The homes were brick or painted white and lots of large sedans sat in the driveways, which suggested to me that retired people lived there. That was good. That meant that the folks might remember Snow, or they might have an idea what happened to her family—or who could have harmed her, whomever that was.

We had driven around on the looping, mazelike streets for a good ten minutes when Snow said. "That's it. That's my old house."

It was similar to the others—made of brick that had been painted white and had black shutters and a cherry-red door. The look of the house was fresh, young. I doubted that her husband still lived there, but you never knew.

"And that's Pam's house," Snow said.

I craned my neck toward the back seat, where she sat. "And why is it that you think we should focus on Pam instead of your husband?"

"Because my husband would've been at work," she said simply. "And Pam was another housewife. If anyone might've seen something, it would've been her, because Pam was always around, one hundred percent of the time."

Well, that made sense. Cammie parked the car, and we stared up at the long ranch-style home. The lawn was freshly mowed and it was nice. But the home hadn't been updated like the one beside it.

There wasn't a vehicle in the driveway. But there was a garage, so it was possible that someone, hopefully Pam, was home.

Cammie shut off the engine and turned to me. "Are you ready? Is Snow ready?"

"I'm ready," Snow said.

I nodded, telling Cammie that she was. "Let's see if Pam is still here and if she has answers."

We got out of the car. The smell of grass filled the air, and the sounds of cicadas buzzing was overwhelming as we made our way up the brick path to the front door.

"Oh, please let Pam be here, please let her be here," Snow whispered.

Cammie rang the bell. After a few seconds, when there was no answer, she knocked hard against the door.

Shuffling came from inside the house. "This is it," Snow said.

The door opened and a familiar face greeted me. "Why hello, Paige. What can I do for you?"

"Mitch Taylor," I said. "What a surprise to see you."

CHAPTER 21

"*W*ho's that?" Snow asked, which I completely ignored. But to be absolutely honest, I was thinking the same thing. What was he doing here? Random coincidence? Or was there more to this?

Perhaps before I got way ahead of myself, I should put my super-sleuth cap away and just have a friendly conversation.

"Hey, Mitch, I don't know if you remember my sister from the reading. This is Cammie."

"How do you do?" he said.

"I do very well indeed. Better now that I've laid eyes on you."

I was a fool to think that my sister was taken so much with Ferguson that she would ignore every other man. She might like the barkeep a lot, but that didn't mean she couldn't appreciate a prime piece of flesh.

Mitch laughed nervously. "Well, ladies, come on in and let's talk."

Inside, the house was a simply decorated. The walls were painted an off-white color, and the accent furnishings were black—ebony cushions on white chairs, black picture frames on white cabinets.

Even though the colors were stark, the place still had a homey feel. I liked it, and it suited Mitch, I thought, what with his research into the darkness of mankind or whatever.

"Place looks different," Snow muttered. "It had more color when Pam lived here."

We sat on a couch, and Mitch took a seat on a leather recliner. "Everything okay, Paige?"

I nodded. "Yes, everything's fine." I wasn't sure how to jump into the previous owner, so I didn't. "Have you heard any updates about Dr. Storm?"

Mitch tsked. "Last I heard, he was still hospitalized. And more people have been, too."

You don't even know. "I heard something about that."

"It's a shame," he said sadly. "A couple of moms called me and said that their kids had fallen ill, and that they were fans."

"Of your books? I know that you feel bad for them."

He covered his mouth with his fist for a moment as if holding back a wall of emotion. "It's just...I'm sure that you can understand this, but my fans mean so much to me. They're like my children. I've given them a tale from which to learn by, and they're supposed to take that lesson out into the world and teach it to others."

I had no idea what he was talking about. I thought that for an author, the *book* was his baby, not the readers. But why kick a dead horse? "I get it. I really do. You're invested in your readers."

"Yes! I am. That's why it's so tragic. It'll make it so hard to write the sequel to *Slasher of Sacrifice.*"

"There's going to be more slashing of teenagers?"

He grinned. "They can never get enough. Here. Look." He jumped up and grabbed a book from a table, bringing it back to me. "This is the original copy of *Slasher.* I had it leather bound and made into its own special edition. Look."

The first page that I turned to was a map of the world. The pages were cream and just a touch darker on the edges, as if they'd been worn by the years.

"This sure is fancy," Cammie said. "You selling these?"

"Oh no." I handed Mitch the copy, and he pressed it to his chest. "I'm not selling this. I had this printed especially for myself. From this book, all the others came."

"I thought that all other books came from a computer," I insisted. "You know, since that's where the book was originally written."

"No, no. *Slasher* was written by hand and then turned into this." He brandished the book again, but this time quickly, so that I just got a flash of the cover. There was something there that I couldn't quite make out. What was that? But before I could see, he spoke again. "That makes it magical to me."

I'd never heard of anything like that—creating one book first and from that the others were made. I didn't even know what that meant.

"Cool," I told him, pretending like I completely understood. Because who wants to look dumb? I wanted to keep the allure of confidence and wisdom that us older women have. "So, Mitch. I'm here for a really strange reason."

He was still staring at the tome in his arms. After a beat he dragged his gaze away. "What's that?"

I cleared my throat, trying to find the words. "There used to be a woman who lived here. Her name was Pam, I believe. I was wondering if you knew anything about her?"

He considered the question. "I've lived here about five years. I don't remember the first name of the folks I bought the place off of, but I recall the last name was Jernigan."

"That's her," Snow said excitedly. "She was Pam Jernigan. Ask if he knows what happened to her."

So I did, and Mitch replied, "She and her husband moved closer to the lake, I think. They'd bought a patch of land on the water and built a house. I've seen her around town a few times. But her husband is sick, so she doesn't come out much, except for things that she needs. And of course, she told me that he was sick five years ago. He may have passed away by now."

"Oh, that would be so sad," Snow mourned. "Mr. Jernigan was nice. I really liked him. He was one of those people who would mow your lawn for you if you needed him to."

Cammie tapped her toe, impatient. "So you cain't tell us any more than that? You don't know where she went?"

Mitch shook his head. "No, sorry, but I can't. Why do you want to know so badly?"

I dismissed him with a wave. "Just an old friend of a—"

"Because she can help us solve a murder," Cammie spit out.

Mitch's brows shot to intrigued peaks. "Murder?"

"She's just kidding. We're not solving any kind of murders." I punched her shoulder. Hard. "What a kidder. You. You're a kidder." Cammie pursed her lips but didn't say anything. I took the opportunity to rise. "Well, Mitch. Thanks so much for your help. We appreciate it."

As we made our way to the door, he added, "You know, there is someone who may be able to help you."

"Who's that?" I asked.

He tapped his fingers to his chin. "If I can just remember her name. I'd seen the two of them talking before—her and Pam. They seemed really close. Ugh. I can't recall. If I think of her name, I'll call you."

"Great. Thank you."

Before he shut the door behind us, Mitch added, "Be careful out there. Lots of strange things going on."

If he only knew. "Will do."

When we were back in the car, Cammie said, "Why'd you shush me about the murder?"

"Because"—I locked my seat belt with a *click*—"Mitch doesn't need to know anything about that. He might…I don't know…think we're doing something bad."

"And what? Call the police on us?"

"Yes," I said tartly in response to her sarcasm. "He might call the police, and to be honest, I don't want to be looked at as a criminal. I've already gone through that."

"Okay," Cammie said glumly. "Whatever you say."

Snow spoke from the back seat. "So Pam's alive. That's great! If only we knew where she lived."

Yes, if only. But we didn't, and gas was too expensive to cruise around the lake looking for her. Besides, the beaches and water features were closed. So. What to do? I pointed the nose of the car back toward home and we set off.

Cammie reached up and grabbed the headrest. "That whole book thing was weird."

I was still thinking about Pam and how to find her. "Hmm?"

"The book? What did he mean that book was the original and all other books came from it?"

I shrugged. "I don't know. Maybe he just meant that was the first one he had printed, so he made it special."

"I don't think so," she murmured. "It didn't seem to be the case."

"What? Are you saying that he actually made that one, and then somehow all the others came from it? Like the book birthed them or something?"

She dropped her hands to her lap with a *thud*. "That's what he suggested, don't you think?"

"How could that even be possible? Books can't come from more books."

Snow piped up. "Maybe he meant that all the other books were copied from the original, like a Xerox."

"Oh, that I get," I said.

"What?" Cammie asked. I told her what Snow had said. My sister nodded enthusiastically. "Yes! All the books were Xeroxed from that one."

I didn't think they'd literally been so, but why disagree? "I bet you're right."

Cammie sat up straight. "Do you know who could help us with that?"

"Who?" I asked, uninterested.

"The librarian," she said proudly.

"What are you talking about?"

"I'm talking about who knows books better than anyone?" Cammie waited. "Well?"

"Am I supposed to answer that?"

"Yes, you are."

Okay, I had no idea where this was going, but I said in an unsure voice, "Um, nobody knows books better than a librarian?"

"Exactly!" She clapped her hands. "No one. So if we want to know all about that book being the original, all we need to do is ask her."

"Why do we care about this so much again?" I was driving us home. We were almost through town. "The library probably isn't open. I'm sure it's closed like most other places."

"No, a library is an essential establishment," Cammie informed me.

No, it wasn't. "Let's just go home."

"There's something about that book," she said. "Something I don't like, and we need to ask that librarian about it."

All I wanted to do was get home and eat a snack. My stomach was grumbling, and a pinch of the smoked cheddar that Cammie had bought on my dime would ease my suffering.

When I didn't reply, she continued, "Please? It'll only take a second."

I sighed. "I don't see why this is important."

"It just is. Trust me."

"Fine." I took the next left and headed us in the direction of the library. When we arrived, there was only one other car in the parking lot. I shot Cammie a contemptuous look. "Essential business, huh?"

"If it's locked up, that's fine. We can come back another day." She shoved open her door. "Come on. Let's get inside."

As we were walking, Snow came up to me. "I think she has a point. I've never heard of a book being the originator."

I didn't answer because there wasn't anything nice to say. This was a wild hair. There wasn't anything to what Mitch had told us, and I didn't understand why Cammie suddenly deemed the whole thing so dang important. It was not a big deal.

The door was unlocked when Cammie pushed it. She flashed me a victorious smile, and I gave her a disgruntled thumbs-up.

"See? Essential business," she told me victoriously.

"Let's just talk to her and go home. This deserted town is starting to creep me out."

It was like being in a zombie apocalypse movie. All the buildings were still standing, but only survivors were walking around.

"She should be back here." Cammie cupped a hand to her mouth. "Oh, librarian! Where are you, librarian?"

Someone kill me now. "Maybe you should keep your voice down."

"Nonsense. There ain't nobody inside," Cammie told me. "Oh, there she is!"

We spotted Vanessa at the same time, hunched over her chair. The woman was probably napping because she was so bored. I did have to hand it to her, though. She was showing up for work while the rest of the world was holed up in their homes.

"Hey, Miss Librarian, we got a question for you." Cammie placed a hand on her shoulder. "Wake up."

Cammie shook her and Vanessa slumped back. Her eyes were open, and she stared vacantly at the ceiling.

Cammie jumped back. "Oh my stars!"

"And garters," Snow exclaimed.

Vanessa had been attacked by whatever was putting people in comas. I pulled out my phone. "We've got to call the ambulance and get her to the hospital."

As I dialed the number, something slipped off Vanessa's lap and fell to the floor.

"A book," Cammie mused. "She was reading up until the end."

My sister retrieved the book and closed it. A familiar arrangement of letters flashed on the cover. Not only that, but I spied a symbol on the cover, the one that had been branded onto the back of the boy's head. I'd seen a sliver of it on Mitch's original copy, too. But I hadn't gotten a good enough look at it to realize that was what it was.

"What's the title?" I asked.

Cammie stiffened as she read, "*Slasher of Sacrifice.*"

My jaw dropped. What were the odds that Vanessa would have been reading Mitch's book when she was attacked?

"Cammie, can you find the page that she'd been reading?"

"Yeah, the book was bent at it." She flipped it open and showed me. "She was reading right here."

My eyes widened as I recognized the passage. Oh. My. Gosh. I might have just solved this mystery.

CHAPTER 22

The ambulance arrived and took Vanessa to the hospital. I dialed Grim's number, but the call went straight to voice mail. I cursed. The one time that I needed him, he was busy. Doing things. Things that were probably important, but that didn't make me feel any better.

"We need a game plan," my sister informed me.

I agreed. The three of us went home to eat and think. Soon as we arrived, I snapped open a bag of smoked cheddar, sliced up a few thin pieces and set them atop hard water crackers.

"Can I have some?" Cammie asked.

"Yes," I replied, though I felt particularly stingy and didn't actually want to give her any. "Eat up."

"I don't understand," Snow said. "What's the book got to do with anything?"

"Grim thought that everything had to do with a monster that came out of the Hieronymus book."

"What are you talking about?" Cammie said.

Oh crap. That was a can of worms I didn't want to open in front of my sister. "Nothing. Sorry."

She glared at me over a slice of smoked cheddar. "Paige, you cain't lie to me. I'm your sister and I know when the truth comes out of your mouth and when you're fibbing."

There were two choices—lie again and hope that I wasn't caught, or fess up. But fessing up had to do with fireworks spewing from hands, and I knew how Cammie felt about that.

Redirect, it was! "We thought that the comas were related to something else. But when you showed me the page in that book, I realized what's going on."

It all made sense. The fact that the patients I'd seen in the hospital looked familiar, that they'd been at the reading, and the passage, it was all clear as day.

"You see—"

My phone chimed. It was Grim. *Finally.* "Hold on," I told Cammie and Snow. "Hey, I've got it figured out."

"Hey," he replied, in his slow, sexy drawl. "You've got what figured out?"

"All of it. Why people are falling into comas."

"Where are you?" he asked.

"Home."

"Hang on tight. I'll be right there."

I hung up the phone. "Grim's on his way. I'm going to keep my theory to myself until he arrives."

Cammie's face bunched in frustration. "You cain't do that! I'm on the edge of my seat!"

"He'll be here shortly."

"Uh! It just figures that I'd have to wait on a man to find out the good stuff."

"I'm going to read the paper until he arrives," Snow said. "Try to remember who it was that Pam was close friends with."

And me, I washed up and made sure to look my Saturday best for Grim. I changed into a slimming pair of jeans and a light cotton shirt, freshened up my makeup, and ran a brush through my hair. There was one thing about being over forty that I couldn't stand—the frizz! I had to spend way more time on my tresses than I'd had to in my twenties and thirties. It was annoying.

So I curled it slightly with the iron, and by the time I finished, there was a knock on the door.

"See," I told Cammie as I headed to answer it, "time went by in a breeze."

"Only for you," she grumbled.

Grim looked tired. He had dark circles under his eyes and a deep scowl on his lips. "Everything okay?" I asked.

"Hard day. Followed up on several leads. Did a lot of tracking but came to nothing."

"What were you tracking, wild animals?" Cammie asked.

"No," he muttered. "Now. What are you thinking?"

I offered him cheese and crackers, which he took with grace, and I talked.

"We found Vanessa, the librarian, today, and she was the same as the others."

"What were you doing at the library?" he asked tersely.

Right. I was supposed to have stayed at home and remained safe after getting Cammie. "Um, well…"

"It was my fault," Cammie said quickly. "I forced Paige into town because I needed to find something out. So if you're going to blame anyone, blame me."

My gaze met my sister's and she smiled slightly. The connection that we'd been working on, the one that had frayed when she stole my credit card, re-formed. I smiled at her, silently thanking her for taking the heat.

Grim paused for a long time before saying, "Then what happened?"

"When we found Vanessa, Mitch Taylor's book fell from her lap. But that wasn't the interesting part. What's important was the page that she'd been reading. You see, Mitch had told me that when he was doing his research, he'd used real incantations that he'd discovered."

Grim quirked a brow. "Real incantations?"

"Right, and I think that's the cause of all the issues. A lot of the people who have been struck by the coma, I saw at the book signing. That can't just be coincidence."

"Hmm," Grim replied, chewing on what I'd told him. "And so you think that this incantation is the problem?"

"Exactly." I snapped my fingers. "It's got to be."

"Does Mitch know about this?" Grim asked.

"That, I don't know. I'm not sure what he realizes and what he doesn't."

"He had that book," Cammie added.

Concern flashed in Grim's eyes. "What book?"

I sighed. *Not this again.* Reluctantly, because I didn't think that book had any real significance in things, I explained about what Mitch considered his original tome, the work that all the others came from.

I finished off with, "But I've never heard of anything like that before," I told Grim. "That a book is the original. Now, there are first publications, and those of antique books can go for so much money. But original works? The first book that bore others? I've never heard of such a thing."

"But you're new to…" Grim started, and I shot him a look that told him not to speak another word.

"New to what?" Cammie asked, eyes flashing with suspicion.

"This town," I told her. "I'm new to this town."

"What's that got to do with anything?" she asked.

"We do things in a different way," he explained. "And an original book is not something that would surprise me in the least."

"Well, *I'm* surprised by the whole thing," Cammie said with a snort. "What you're talking about, Paige, with the whole incantation stuff, sounds like the devil's work."

How to put this gently? "Well, Cammie, I know it sounds crazy, but people have been working spells for centuries. It could be the devil's work. I don't know. But what I do know is that people are falling victim to a coma, one that science can't explain. The words in that book are powerful, so powerful that I believe it's the cause of the crisis in town."

"But how're you going to stop it?" Cammie asked. "It's a book, and books are available everywhere. Everybody knows that."

"The original book," Grim murmured.

All gazes lashed on him. "What?" I asked.

He scraped a hand down the stubble of his cheek. The five-o'clock shadow that peppered his jawline looked good enough to lick. Wait. Sorry. I was supposed to be thinking about how to stop the rest of our town, if not the state, from succumbing to a coma that had no cure. I wasn't supposed to be thinking about how delicious Grim looked.

Besides, he didn't want to get attached.

A twinge of hurt tweaked my stomach. I tried to ignore it, but the ache throbbed more.

It was no big deal. I didn't have time to get attached to anyone, anyway.

"The book that you say Mitch has," Grim continued. "If it's what I call an originator book, then possibly by destroying that, we can eliminate all traces of the novel everywhere."

"Let me see for a second," Cammie said. She grabbed her phone and scrolled through it. "Yep. Just what I thought. Mitch's book is available online, too. How're you going to get rid of those copies?"

"Same way," Grim said. "By destroying that book."

She frowned. "I don't think that's how that works. I'm pretty sure somebody sat at a big mahogany desk and uploaded a file and added a description of the book. You cain't just get rid of a physical copy and it'll remove something on an online bookstore site."

Oh yes, he could. "Let Grim and I worry about that. The main thing that we need to do right now is stop anyone else from succumbing to the curse."

"I'm on it," Cammie said.

What exactly, was she on? She thumbed on her phone and stared at me. "Well?"

"Well, what?"

"What's Mitch's number?"

"You can't just call him."

"Why cain't I? We need that book. He's got it. Sounds like a win-win to me."

"She's right." Grim crossed to me and stood really close, like so close that I could feel his body heat rolling off him in waves and lapping against my body. I never wanted to move again. "We need Mitch to bring that book to us."

"What if he won't?" I said. "What if he knows that he's responsible for everything that's going on, and he doesn't want it to stop?"

"Then you go bang-bang," Cammie said, nodding toward her purse.

For goodness' sake. You couldn't just go around shooting people. "That's not a solution."

She shrugged, unconvinced.

"It's possible," Grim told us, "that he knows exactly what he's done, and because of the celebrity that the book offers, he doesn't care."

"And it's also possible that he doesn't know," I argued. "Mitch Taylor does not strike me as the sort of person who would deliberately harm people."

"You wouldn't believe the things that folks'll do for money." Cammie rubbed her arms as if a chill had set into her bones. "You just wouldn't."

My internal alarm blared inside my head. What did that mean? What was Cammie talking about?

But this wasn't the time to hatch that out. So instead of prying, I offered her a lifeline. "Well, whatever a person does for money, sometimes it may seem like the right decision at that time."

She nodded but didn't look at me.

"Our first priority," Grim said, "is getting that book and seeing if your theory is true, that it is the cause of our problems here. To do that, we've got to talk to Mitch. Where can I find him?"

I started to tell Grim where Mitch was just as my phone started ringing. I let it go to voice mail, and it started up again. *Sheesh*. Who needed to get in touch with me so desperately?

"You going to answer that?" Grim asked.

It might have been Madeleine. Just what I needed, to discuss my career when everyone was falling victim to a magical coma that no one knew how to break.

I pulled my phone from my purse and glanced at it. My heart nearly jumped from my chest.

"Y'all." I slowly held up the phone for them to see. "We might not have to go to Mitch. We may be able to bring him to us."

Because dialing me at that moment was Mitch Taylor.

CHAPTER 23

"Answer it," Grim instructed. "Get him to bring the book somewhere."

"Where?"

"My house."

I shot him a startled look. "Your house? Why?"

"Because," he murmured in my ear, making my skin buzz with want, "I have things there that can help us."

"You mean, like an arsenal of weapons in case the little nerd comes prepared?" Cammie asked.

"Yep," I said dryly, "just like that."

"Maybe you can sic a team of ghosts on his butt," my sister offered enthusiastically.

Grim looked like he wanted to ask a question about that, but shook his head instead. "You may want to answer that before he gets away."

I thumbed on the phone. "Hello?"

"Paige, hi, it's Mitch Taylor."

"Hi Mitch. How're you?"

"Just fine. Look, I thought of the person who knew Pam, who I've seen her with."

"Great. Can we meet to chat about it?"

Mitch paused. "I thought you'd just want the information over the phone."

"Sorry, the connection is so bad." I made a static sound with my voice. "You're cutting in and out. Listen, my friend really wants to read your book, and I told him about the original copy. He's a..."

I shot Grim a frantic glance and he said, "Book dealer."

Awesome! "He deals in collectible books, and he said that maybe yours could fetch a huge price. He'd love to see it."

"I don't know," Mitch started.

I made the static sound again. "Terrible connection. Meet me at"—I gave him the address—"and we can discuss Pam. Bring the book."

Then I hung up and exhaled. My heart was beating a thousand times a minute. "Well, that's over. Now all we have to do is wait."

"No. All we have to do is get to my place. You can ride with me."

As I moved to go with Grim, Cammie said in a tinny voice, "What about me? What am I supposed to do?"

"Stay here," I told her. "I'll call you when it's over."

She frowned. "Why do you get to have all the fun?"

"Because that's how it goes this time around. This time, the younger sister gets to be the one in charge. Don't leave. Not until I get back. You got it?"

Cammie gave me a mock salute. "Aye, aye, captain."

WE ARRIVED at Grim's house within minutes. I didn't know if Mitch would actually show. After all, he might've figured I was lying about the static. But the thought of millions of dollars for a single book could be enough to wet his interest.

"What are we going to do?" I asked Grim.

He shot me a hard look. "*I* am going to speak with Mitch and look at the book. *I* am also going to get a gauge on whether or not he's aware that the book could be behind this town's mystery. *I* am also going to decipher the magic in the spell and see if it's dark enough and strong enough to paralyze people into comas."

There were an awful lot of *I*'s in his words. "You can't read the incantation. That's where it gets you. It may have some kind of lag time on it, too. Because neither Lulu nor Dr. Storm had the book on them when I found them."

"It may take a while to work in some people and also work immediately in others. Like how medicine is. Some folks are affected quickly by some prescription drugs, while others don't feel the effects until later. It's a body chemistry thing."

"Got it." I folded my arms. "And while you're doing all those things that are only for you, what am I supposed to be doing?"

"Staying out of the way."

I scoffed. "I do not like your tone or your instructions."

"Look—"

A knock came from the door. I shot Grim a victorious glance. Now he didn't have time to tell me why he wanted to keep Baby in the corner. I could play a bigger role and maybe even use my magic if I had to.

Grim opened the door and thrust out his hand. He even smiled. What a rare sight. "Mitch Taylor, great to meet you. My name's Grim."

Mitch smiled nervously. The book was nowhere in sight, but he did have a backpack strap slung over his shoulder. "Is there anything more to your name? Do I call you Mr. Grim?"

"Nope. Just Grim. Come on in."

"Paige," Mitch said.

"So glad you found the place."

"Please, sit." Grim gestured to the couch.

Savage came out from wherever he'd been hiding and gave Mitch's hand a friendly lick. "Nice dog," he murmured.

I realized that Mitch couldn't see the wings. He wasn't magical.

"Savage, go back to your spot."

Under Grim's instruction, the dog went back to wherever his spot was. Grim followed Savage and shut a door. He returned, rubbing his hands together and smiling.

"Paige tells me that you have a book, an original copy. I'd love to see it as I trade in that sort of thing."

"Well," Mitch started, "I'm not sure that it's going to be worth much. The book was just published."

"Oh, you can never be too sure about these things," Grim lied. "Often people will buy a book simply because it is the original. May I have a look?"

Mitch stared at Grim's outstretched hand with worry. A long pause ensued. Just as sweat sprouted on my brow, Mitch unzipped the backpack and pulled out *Slasher of Sacrifice*.

"Here it is."

Grim grabbed it. "Ah a beautiful specimen. May I see it?"

Mitch handed the book over, and while Grim leafed through the pages, the author turned to me. "I didn't expect all this excitement. And to be honest, I was worried about driving over here. But I guess the police are more concerned that people stay away from the lake than drive through the streets."

"They have their hands full," I replied.

"Yes, and like I said over the phone, I remember who was good friends with Pam."

"Right. Who was that?"

"This is a great book. Paige, wasn't there something you wanted to show me?" Grim asked.

I was dying to know who Pam had been friends with, but helping Grim was important, too. I took the book and flipped through it until I found the incantation. "This is it."

Grim rose and said to Mitch, "Is it okay if I take a closer look at my work station?"

"As long as you don't destroy it," Mitch said with a laugh.

If he only knew.

"It'll be perfectly safe. Be right back."

As Grim disappeared into his rainforest, worry gripped me. What if something did happen to him? I'd explained not to read the incantation, but what if he couldn't help himself? Curiosity killed the cat, after all.

The best way to deal with worry was diversion, so I turned back to Mitch. "You were saying about who knew Pam?"

Mitch, who appeared lost in thought, snapped back to attention. "Yes! Sorry, I got distracted there for a moment." He rose and took a step toward the room that Grim had disappeared into. "You don't think he'll do anything to mess up the original, do you?"

"No, of course not," I told him. "He only wants to ascertain its value."

Mitch nodded absently. "It's valuable to me, but I don't know about to anyone else. It's just…there are things that I'm uncertain of, things that I worry about. I don't know if it's just in my head or if it's real."

Oh, it's real, buddy. "You have nothing to worry about. Grim will take very good care of it. Like I said, it's about the value, nothing else. But you were saying about Pam?"

Could we please get back to Pam? I wanted a jackpot of information to be able to take back to Snow. This could be the lead that she needed that would start us down the path of what happened to her.

"Right, Pam." He flashed me that thousand-watt smile of his. "Yes, the woman that I saw her talking with was—"

"Paige, could I see you for a minute?" Grim said.

What in the world? Didn't he know that he was interrupting an important conversation? "Hold that thought," I told Mitch before scuttling over to Grim.

He pulled me inside the greenhouse, which chirped with life. "It's true," he whispered, "everything that you've thought. The book is powerful, and it's the original source of all the trouble here."

I blinked in surprise. "Wow. You deciphered all of that, that quickly?"

He nodded grimly. Ha. I made a joke. Get it? Grim nodded grimly? "It didn't take much to figure it out, no. Power is leaking out of it. Look."

He pointed to where it lay on his workbench, and sure enough, you could see the magic floating off it in the form of purple fog.

"So what do we do?" I asked.

"Destroy it. There's no other way. We get rid of it and then people will awaken from their comas and we'll stop anyone else from being cursed."

"What about Mitch?" I said.

"I'll offer to buy the book," Grim replied. "Then I'll do it."

"And if he says no?"

Grim's chiseled jawline hardened to stone. "Then things get complicated."

I patted his shoulder. "I'm not worried about you. If you can handle monsters, then you can handle one man. Let's go in and talk to him."

We turned to head into the living room and were surprised to see Mitch standing in the doorway. He had a gun leveled at us. "Destroy my book? Over your dead bodies."

CHAPTER 24

*M*itch took the book from where it had been sitting atop the table. "I'll take that, thank you very much."

I immediately went into book tour public relations mode, putting on my biggest smile. "Mitch, I don't know if you realize this, but your book is harming people—literally. It's causing your friends, like Dr. Storm, to fall into a coma. Even your fans are succumbing to it, and as far as we know, there's no cure. No one has snapped out of it yet."

He shrugged. "It's a small price to pay for fame."

"What has celebrity done to you people?" Grim asked. "You get one taste and have to drink from the entire vat of the mixture."

"It's addictive," I confirmed.

"I worked years on that book," Mitch admitted. "Dr. Storm helped me find the incantation. I knew the possibilities of what it could do, what would happen. Since I wrote it down and created the origin book, then I was immune to its effects. Yes, there was always the risk that people would fall into comas, but look at my sales!"

He opened an app on his phone and showed us an upward trajectory line in real time of how many books that he'd sold. "I'm famous. I've done it! I've reached my ultimate goal!"

"As great as that is," I told him, "you're harming people. I understand what it is to have worked your entire life toward something, I really do. But your fame and fortune can't be put above other people's wellness."

"Oh yes, it can," he said. "Thank you for trying to be altruistic. But we're talking about my livelihood. And like I said, my book will never be destroyed. It was nice meeting you, Paige. I appreciate what you did for me, coming to the book signing, but this is where we part."

Mitch raised the gun. Quick as lightning, Grim lifted his hand, and a bolt of lightning shot out, hitting the weapon. The gun fired and Grim grunted, falling back.

I reached for him. "No!"

His gaze met mine. "Stop him."

What? How was I supposed to stop Mitch? He had a gun. I had... powers that I couldn't control and had to meditate in a yoga-like pose in order to summon them. What good was I in this situation?

Mitch trained the gun on me. "I didn't do well with that shot, but I can get this next one just right."

As he closed in, fear gripped me. I could either stand put and die, or I could move.

Suddenly my feet were moving straight for him. I barreled into Mitch's chest. He stumbled backward and the book fell from his grasp.

It wasn't the gun, but it was good enough. I grabbed the book and raced into the greenhouse, no clue what I was doing. Why was I running farther inside the greenhouse? Was there an escape? I felt like a dimwitted heroine in a horror movie. This was the scene when she was trapped inside the house. Instead of running toward the front door, like any normal human being, she ran up the stairs, where there was no chance for escape.

That was me. Right now.

I hid behind some foliage and hoped no little critters jumped out and bit me.

"Come out, come out, wherever you are," Mitch called.

No, thank you. I could hear him walking the path, closing in. My heartbeat jumped into my throat, flapping like a hummingbird's wings. I was backed into a corner, with no escape.

To one side of me there were plants, on the other were a row of Grim's books. That gave me an idea.

"There you are," Mitch said, gun leveled at me.

"Mitch, don't do this," I told him, rising. "Just take the book and go."

"And let you tell the rest of the world about what I've done? Not a chance. Hand it over or I'll shoot your hand."

I gave him the book, which he didn't even look at as he clutched it to his chest. "Thank you. Now I'm afraid to say that our relationship has come to an—"

Before he could finish his sentence, one of the little leaf-like creatures jumped onto Mitch's head.

Mitch jerked back. "What in the world?"

He pinched the creature between his thumb and forefinger and lowered it to eye level. Mitch took one look at it and screamed.

That must've been the signal, because a hundred of those little guys rushed from the foliage and attacked Mitch.

He screamed and raced toward the greenhouse door. I followed, working to find my magic as he ran. It swirled like a summer storm in my belly, and I felt lightning prick my fingertips.

As Mitch made his way to the front greenhouse door, little creatures fell off him, scampering back into the foliage that they'd come from. I held my breath as Mitch closed in.

"Three...two...one."

Mitch reached the door and attempted to run through, but the book he was holding, the one that looked so much like his original copy of *Slasher of Sacrifice* but wasn't, hit the barrier to the greenhouse and flew back into the room while Mitch plummeted forward, hitting the ground with a thud.

The gun had flown out of Mitch's hand. I raced forward, feeling my boobs and butt jiggling a little more than I'd like, scooped it up, and reached Mitch just as he was coming to from hitting the back of his head against the floor.

"What...what happened?"

I aimed the barrel at him. "Mitch Taylor, I'm afraid to say it, but you've just written your last chapter."

Grim appeared at the door. He smiled wanly. Then he grunted. That seemed about right. "Keep your gun on him while I call this in."

I eyed him. "What're you going to call in, exactly? He hasn't killed anyone."

Grim shook his head. "He tried to kill us."

"Oh, right."

"And also"—Grim held the original copy of *Slasher* in his hand—"this has to go."

He grimaced in pain as he pointed one finger at it and the book erupted into flames.

"No," Mitch screamed. "How did you do that?"

Grim ignored him. "I'll call Cowan."

While Grim did that, Mitch Taylor lay on the floor and cried.

CHAPTER 25

Mitch was arrested and charged with attempted murder. When Cowan asked Grim what that was about, he explained the entire situation to the officer.

Cowan scratched the baby-fine hairs atop his head. "So I guess there wasn't a monster running around after all, was there?"

Grim just grunted in response.

He had been shot, just below the shoulder. The pain had thrown him for a loop for a bit, but he'd come through at the end, up and ready to help me. He was a big man, and the wound wasn't that large, which made me suspect something.

"You just wanted to see if I could work my powers without your help, didn't you?"

"I don't know what you're talking about," he replied.

I smirked. "I think you do. But never mind. I managed not to die."

"You outsmarted him," he said with what I suspected was a tinge of pride to his voice.

"Grim, are you impressed with me?"

His mouth split into a smile. "I would say that I am."

"Wait. We've got to get you to a doctor. You've got to get the bullet removed."

He shrugged.

"What?"

"I may have healed myself."

"*What?*"

Grim pulled back his shirt and showed me that the wound was gone.

"Who are you, a superhero? Are you really Hugh Jackman playing Wolverine and have a healing power?"

"I just used magic."

Now I was super suspicious. "When?"

"You had it handled."

"Grim, I could've been shot."

He shook his head. "I wouldn't have let that happen."

He'd just admitted that he healed himself while we were still in the greenhouse with an armed Mitch. I didn't know if I should've been furious or proud that he thought I could handle the situation.

"You've got a lot of will in you," he told me.

Not sure if I felt better.

As Mitch was being taken away in handcuffs, he called out, "Her name's Patricia. She owns lots of rental homes. The woman Pam is friends with."

I'd almost forgotten. To Grim I said, "That was so nice of him to remember what it was we'd been talking about."

"Yeah, nice people put others in comas all the time," he said dryly.

"I didn't say *he* was nice. Just that what he did right then, was."

Another grunt from team Grim. "Come on. Let's get you home."

"Wait. We have to go to the hospital first."

He quirked a brow. "Hospital?"

"To see if folks are coming out of their comas."

He nodded. "Come on."

We reached the hospital a few minutes later. The first person I wanted to check on was Dr. Storm. We arrived at his room just as his wife was saying, "It's a miracle. He's awake."

Not wanting to disturb them, I peeked in to see the professor's eyes wide open and him replying to the nurse who'd just walked in and asked him how he felt.

That was how it was through the rest of the building. People were waking up. It filled my heart with warm fuzzies.

"And what about his digital books?" I wondered aloud.

"Look and see," Grim told me.

I pulled up the online bookstore and searched for Mitch Taylor and his book, but nothing appeared. "Looks like when we destroyed the original, we got rid of all the copies."

"Good," was all Grim said.

I supposed it was enough and that it reflected how I felt inside. Good. It was done. The drama was over and life could resume.

GRIM TOOK me home and I told Cammie and Snow everything that had happened.

"And Mitch remembered who knew Pam. It's Patricia, my landlady. She's in Hawaii right now, but maybe we can call her tomorrow."

"Thank you," Snow said.

I smiled. "I just hope we can get some answers for you."

Cammie yawned. "I don't know about y'all, but I'm pooped. All this sleuthing has worn me out."

I chuckled. "All this sleuthing, huh?"

"Yep. I'm fatigued and got to get my beauty sleep so that I can be ready to go in the morning."

"Oh? You got a long drive ahead of you?" I asked, wondering if she was leaving, if her *stay*cation at my rental was done.

"Nah, just wanting to get back to hanging out with Ferguson."

Okay. Well, there was my answer.

"And," Cammie added, "I'm still on my mission to put the Southern back into you."

I rolled my eyes. "What are we gonna do, go frog gigging or something?"

"Not a bad plan," she said.

She yawned again and I said my good nights, heading into my room to change and sleep. My eyes shut as soon as my head hit the pillow, and they didn't open again until sunlight streamed through my windows.

The next day when I went into town, life was back to normal. The police had announced that the lake was safe and that closing it had been a big misunderstanding. Apparently people believed them and raced back to the lake because the shops and stores were busy. I spotted several people that I knew, including Lulu and Vanessa, the librarian.

It was good to see them out again, wandering the streets and living their best lives.

I smiled as I approached the Gnome Grill, which was the Gone Grill to humans. Sitting outside on the patio was Grim. He stood and kissed my cheek when I arrived. He also made sure to brush his hand against mine.

"Thank you for having lunch with me," he murmured in that sexy growl of his.

"Thank you for inviting me." He stared at me for a long moment, so long that my cheeks heated. "What is it? Is there something on my nose?"

"No. I just like looking at you."

I definitely blushed then and we enjoyed a nice lunch, though I still wasn't sure exactly where our relationship was going. But for now that was okay. If he didn't get too invested, I wouldn't, either.

When lunch was finished, I'd promised Snow that I'd call Patricia as soon as I felt that it was a decent time in Hawaii. I headed home to keep that promise.

When I arrived, I saw no signs of Snow, and I heard Cammie in the bathroom.

She must've heard the front door open because she shouted, "Hey, Paige, I'll be right out!"

"Okay. But no rush, I don't need to go."

She'd left her black duffel bag open on the couch. Her clothes were hanging out of it. I rolled my eyes. Would my sister never learn to clean up after herself?

"Cammie, your stuff's everywhere."

"I'll get it," she called. "Just leave it."

But there was a pair of panties touching the couch. Yuck. I grabbed a pair of thongs from the kitchen and moved to pick them up when the thongs slipped from my fingers and clattered to the floor.

I barely heard the bathroom door open. "Oh crap."

My body tingled from head to foot. I pointed to the bag and slowly said to my sister, "Where did all that money come from?"

There were hundreds of one-hundred-dollar bills wrapped in bank tape. Handfuls—more than handfuls. There were so many bills I couldn't even guess how many there were.

"Cammie," I warned. "What's going on?"

She cringed. "You see, Paige. I may have done something very bad."

I folded my arms. "Start talking. Right now."

"You might want to sit down for this."

And sit down for her story, I did.

Why does Cammie have a duffel bag full of cash? What sort of trouble is she in?
Find out in SPELL, DON'T TELL!
Click HERE to order.

If you never want to miss a release, be sure to sign up for my newsletter. You'll have access to sneak peaks of books and will be notified whenever I'm running a sale! Click HERE.

And join my private Facebook Group, the Bless Your Witch club. There, we chat about books and get to know one another. You'll get to do fun things like vote on covers and read unedited chapters. You'll be the first to know insider info. You can join HERE.

ALSO BY AMY BOYLES

SERIES READING ORDER

A MAGICAL RENOVATION MYSERY

WITCHER UPPER

RENOVATION SPELL

DEMOLITION PREMONITION

WITCHER UPPER CHRISTMAS

BARN BEWITCHMENT

SHIPLAP AND SPELL HUNTING

MUDROOM MYSTIC

WITCH IT OR LIST IT

PANTRY PRANKSTER

HOME TOWN MAGIC

WITCH APPEAL

WHITE MAGIC AND WARDROBES

LOST SOUTHERN MAGIC

(Takes place following the events of Southern Magic Wedding. This is a Sweet Tea Witches, Southern Belles and Spells, Southern Ghost Wrangles and Bless Your Witch Crossover)

THE GOLD TOUCH THAT WENT CATTYWAMPUS

THE YELLOW-BELLIED SCAREDY CAT

A MESS OF SIRENS

KNEE-HIGH TO A THIEF

BELLES AND SPELLS MATCHMAKER MYSTERY

DEADLY SPELLS AND A SOUTHERN BELLE

CURSED BRIDES AND ALIBIS

MAGICAL DAMES AND DATING GAMES

SOME PIG AND A MUMMY DIG

SWEET TEA WITCH MYSTERIES
SOUTHERN MAGIC
SOUTHERN SPELLS
SOUTHERN MYTHS
SOUTHERN SORCERY
SOUTHERN CURSES
SOUTHERN KARMA
SOUTHERN MAGIC THANKSGIVING
SOUTHERN MAGIC CHRISTMAS
SOUTHERN POTIONS
SOUTHERN FORTUNES
SOUTHERN HAUNTINGS
SOUTHERN WANDS
SOUTHERN CONJURING
SOUTHERN WISHES
SOUTHERN DREAMS
SOUTHERN MAGIC WEDDING
SOUTHERN OMENS
SOUTHERN JINXED
SOUTHERN BEGINNINGS
SOUTHERN MYSTICS
SOUTHERN CAULDRONS
SOUTHERN HOLIDAY
SOUTHERN ENCHANTED
SOUTHERN TRAPPINGS

THE ACCIDENTAL MEDIUM
WITCH'S BLOCK
POISONED PROSE
SPELL, DON'T TELL

SOUTHERN GHOST WRANGLER MYSTERIES

SOUL FOOD SPIRITS

HONEYSUCKLE HAUNTING

THE GHOST WHO ATE GRITS (Crossover with Pepper and Axel from Sweet Tea Witches)

BACKWOODS BANSHEE

MISTLETOE AND SPIRITS

BLESS YOUR WITCH SERIES

SCARED WITCHLESS

KISS MY WITCH

QUEEN WITCH

QUIT YOUR WITCHIN'

FOR WITCH'S SAKE

DON'T GIVE A WITCH

WITCH MY GRITS

FRIED GREEN WITCH

SOUTHERN WITCHING

Y'ALL WITCHES

HOLD YOUR WITCHES

SOUTHERN SINGLE MOM PARANORMAL MYSTERIES

The Witch's Handbook to Hunting Vampires

The Witch's Handbook to Catching Werewolves

The Witch's Handbook to Trapping Demons

ABOUT THE AUTHOR

Hey, I'm Amy,

I write books for folks who crave laugh-out-loud paranormal mysteries. I help bring humor into readers' lives. I've got a Pharm D in pharmacy, a BA in Creative Writing and a Masters in Life.

And when I'm not writing or chasing around two kids (one of which is seven going on seventeen), I can be found antique shopping for a great deal, getting my roots touched up (because that's an every four week job) and figuring out when I can get back to Disney World.

If you're dying to know more about my wacky life, here are three things you don't know about me.

—In college I spent a semester at Marvel Comics working in the X-Men office.

—I worked at Carnegie Hall.

—I grew up in a barbecue restaurant—literally. My parents owned one.

If you want to reach out to me—and I love to hear from readers—you can email me at amyboylesauthor@gmail.com.

Happy reading!

Printed in Great Britain
by Amazon

20071410R10092